Kinda Don't Care

Book 1 of The Simple Man Series

By

Lani Lynn Vale

ISBN-13:
978-1986697415

ISBN-10:
198669741X

Dedication

Right now, my eyes are drooping, and I'm on a low-calorie diet. How does one expect me to write a dedication? I suck at them, and now my brain hurts.

I think I'll dedicate this book to the cookie I'm going to demolish—because I have zero willpower.

Acknowledgements

Model- Joey Berry

Photographer: Furiousfotog

Cover Designer: Cover Me Darling

Editors: Gray Ink and Ink It Out Editing

Content Editor: Danielle Palumbo

Leah Michelle, Barbara New, Kathy West, Laura Green, Mindy Kugler, Diane Swenson, Kendra LaSalle—my betas—y'all are the best. I love each and every one of you!

Lori Vale, my mom and second pair of eyes—I couldn't write without you. <3

CONTENTS

Prologue- Page 9
Prologue- Page 11
Chapter 1- Page 15
Chapter 2- Page 37
Chapter 3- Page 45
Chapter 4- Page 67
Chapter 5- Page 71
Chapter 6- Page 91
Chapter 7- Page 103
Chapter 8- Page 109
Chapter 9- Page 121
Chapter 10- Page 131
Chapter 11- Page 137
Chapter 12- Page 159
Chapter 13- Page 165
Chapter 14- Page 173
Chapter 15- Page 179
Chapter 16- Page 191
Chapter 17- Page 205
Chapter 18- Page 233
Chapter 19- Page 245
Chapter 20- Page 259
Chapter 21- Page 271
Chapter 22- Page 277
Chapter 23- Page 299
Chapter 24- Page 311
Epilogue- Page 317

Other titles by Lani Lynn Vale:

The Freebirds

Boomtown

Highway Don't Care

Another One Bites the Dust

Last Day of My Life

Texas Tornado

I Don't Dance

The Heroes of The Dixie Wardens MC

Lights To My Siren

Halligan To My Axe

Kevlar To My Vest

Keys To My Cuffs

Life To My Flight

Charge To My Line

Counter To My Intelligence

Right To My Wrong

Code 11- KPD SWAT

Center Mass

Double Tap

Bang Switch

Execution Style

Charlie Foxtrot

Kill Shot

Coup De Grace

The Uncertain Saints

Whiskey Neat

Jack & Coke

Vodka On The Rocks

Bad Apple

Dirty Mother

Rusty Nail

The Kilgore Fire Series

Shock Advised

Flash Point

Oxygen Deprived

Controlled Burn

Put Out

I Like Big Dragons Series

I Like Big Dragons and I Cannot Lie

Dragons Need Love, Too

Oh, My Dragon

The Dixie Warden Rejects

Beard Mode

Fear the Beard

Son of a Beard

I'm Only Here for the Beard

The Beard Made Me Do It

Beard Up

For the Love of Beard

Law & Beard

There's No Crying in Baseball
Pitch Please

Quit Your Pitchin'

The Hail Raisers
Hail No

Go to Hail

Burn in Hail

What the Hail

The Hail You Say

Hail Mary

The Simple Man Series

Kinda Don't Care

PROLOGUE

Gave that bitch a wedding. Bitches love weddings.

Rafe

The first time I saw her, she said she was sorry I only had one ball.

The second time was a year later, bloody and bruised. She said she was sorry that my face looked like someone had taken a bat to it.

The third, I'd arrived with information that the Freebirds organization might want to hear, and I had earned myself a place in their infrastructure that would solidify our relationship for years to come. She'd been having a sleepover with her friends. Seven fifteen-year-old girls. I couldn't get out of there fast enough.

The fourth, a year after the last time, I'd walked in and felt like I'd been punched in the stomach. Because between the previous visit and the latest visit, she'd shed her baby skin and was blossoming into the beautiful young woman she would one day become.

The fifth and sixth times had been over the course of the next five years. From the day that I'd felt that kick to the gut, I'd done my level best to stay away. If I had to go over to the Free compound, I went in the dead of night, visited with the boys and left. But, she'd caught me leaving both times—and both of those times she had been even prettier than she was the previous time.

The seventh time was two years after that when I had been coming home from a spec ops mission. I was dressed in my camo BTUs just like all the other soldiers who were returning home. I wasn't actually a soldier. Not anymore, at least. I'd been there, working amongst other soldiers, on a classified operation posing as a soldier in an attempt to ascertain who the hell was the contact point behind a rash of stolen military paraphernalia.

She'd been standing there, smiling and waving, welcoming soldiers home.

It'd been the turning point for me.

No longer was she underage. No longer was I going to hide.

I couldn't get her out of my mind. I couldn't, and I should have.

But, the heart works in mysterious ways.

I didn't get to choose who I loved. Who I wanted.

And, had things not turned south? Well, we might've both gotten what we wanted.

The hardest part of all, though, was forgetting she ever existed in the first place.

Oh, and that one night we spent together.

PROLOGUE II

*Thanks to breast implants, if there ever was a zombie apocalypse,
there'd be a few with some fine ass titties.*
-Janie to Kayla

James

"You're not going," I flat out refused. "You're not. You're…"

"I'm an adult, Dad!" Janie, my daughter who was indeed an adult, screamed. "You can't stop me!"

"It's fucking night time," I snapped. "You're not going to find a goddamn thing at night."

Janie was shaking in anger as she stared at me with a look I'd never seen cross her face before right then. "He was shot. He could have drowned. I can't leave him out there. I have to know."

My daughter's friend, who happened to be a forty-one-year-old man named Rafe, was missing.

Earlier in the day, he'd been in an altercation. Earlier in the day, he'd been hurt. Earlier in the day, he'd then gone to help a woman who was drowning in her car—which had been purposefully pushed over a bridge with her child inside.

Then, somewhere after the woman and her child were saved, Rafe went under. Rafe, for all intents and purposes, died.

At least in the eyes of all the other search crews.

We'd arrived from our hometown of Kilgore, Texas to help in the search. But, after hearing of Rafe's gunshot wound—which, according to the man who had helped Rafe save the woman, had been fairly serious—it was determined that Rafe had passed out in the water and had died.

The banks had been searched. The immediate area dragged by boats. The area surrounding the river had been searched.

Literally, the only thing left was for the remaining part of the river to be dragged.

There was nowhere else he *could* be.

They'd searched twenty miles of river and bank. There was no way he was alive.

None.

And Janie knew it.

"Daddy…"

My heart broke, and I wrapped my arms around her shoulders, pulling her into my chest as I'd done a hundred thousand times over the course of her young life.

"I'm sorry, baby."

An altercation in the hallway beyond the stairwell we were standing in had me glancing up through the tiny window, and what I saw made my heart stop.

But, as if the universe was laughing at me, the man himself came falling out of the elevator.

He was wet. He had blood running down his face and pooling in the collar of his shirt, and he looked about ready to pass out.

He did pass out.

He hit the ground about two steps outside of the elevator.

I reached for the stairwell door, and it didn't take my daughter long to hear the commotion, and the name that everybody was screaming.

She stiffened in my arms, and then bolted.

"Rafe!" Janie cried. "Oh my God! Rafe!"

And, as I watched my daughter land on her knees beside the man who I always suspected wasn't just a friend, I realized a few things.

One, my daughter was in love with a man that was almost twenty years older than her.

Two, Rafe was going to die—by my hand—if he ever hurt her.

And three, this could go nowhere good.

Especially, I realized, hours later when we found out that Rafe didn't remember any of the last six months. Meaning, the period of time in which he and my daughter had grown the closest. Nearly choking on my spit at where my thoughts were going, it occurred to me that they've obviously become more to each other than I ever expected.

Janie was devastated—beyond broken.

I had a feeling I didn't have the entire story.

CHAPTER 1

You look like duct tape and handcuff material.
-Things you shouldn't say to a man you have a crush on

Janie

The day Rafe no longer saw me as forbidden.

I watched the airport terminal, my belly jostling with nerves.

Rafe would be there soon.

I'd been looking his name up on flight manifests trying to figure out where he was at least once every three or four days. (Yes, I knew I was obsessed.) But, since I had no clue where he was going, I'd started searching specifically for his name, even though I always wondered if he had an alias.

I'd known, of course, that he was going to be there. But honestly, from day-to-day, I wasn't quite sure what exactly it was that Rafe did.

Though, this time I'd gotten a little help from the man himself—albeit inadvertently seeing as he hadn't actually given me the information. He'd given it to my Uncle Sam—not the government Uncle Sam, but my actual Uncle Sam.

A girl had to do what a girl had to do if she wanted to see the man she'd fallen in love with, after all. Even steal information off of her Uncle's desk.

It seemed like one day Rafe was home on American soil, working as a liaison between three governmental agencies, and the next he was deployed.

No matter how hard I tried, I could never find anything out about the man. He was too good at hiding.

Jack, my pseudo-uncle and mentor, and his wife, Winter, had taught me everything I knew about computers, and now there was literally nothing I couldn't find out if I put my mind to it.

Nothing, that was, unless it came to Raphael Luis.

I had no fucking clue why I couldn't find anything on him.

Literally, there was absolutely no information that was safe. There was nothing that I couldn't find out. I knew that my dad was once a porn-aholic before he'd met Shiloh—which happened to be over twenty years ago. I'd been on his old computer trying to figure out how to get into the hard drive and had unfortunately discovered that interesting tidbit, something that no girl wants to know about her father. I also knew that my little sister was talking in some nerd chatroom all hours of the night and apparently had a secret boyfriend that she was keeping from my father.

I knew that there were quite a few people in town who were curious enough to Google Free, the organization that Uncle Sam— again, my actual Uncle Sam, not the literal Uncle Sam—had started with my father and the rest of my pseudo-uncles. They wanted to know more, and I understood their curiosity. But to protect Free and the women we helped, I pointed them in a direction that wouldn't give them any more information than what the rest of the population could come up with.

For that organization that my family had created—the one for which I now worked—I basically did what Uncle Jack and Aunt Winter did, just on a much broader scale.

I'd surpassed the masters, but I still had such a thirst for knowledge that I continued to push myself.

Which was why it was so frustrating that I couldn't find a damn thing on Rafe.

Not a single, solitary thing.

The fact that I could find nothing on the man was disconcerting.

Not a birth certificate. No social security number. Not even his high school baseball pictures.

Someone jostled me, and I looked to the side to see a very pregnant woman shifting from foot-to-foot. "I'm sorry. I think I'm in labor. My balance is a little off."

I smiled and scooted away slightly, causing her to laugh.

"It's not contagious," she teased.

I shrugged.

Maybe I didn't want her water breaking all over my shoes. I knew quite a bit of medical related information, and usually when one was in labor, their water broke.

Just sayin'.

"Who are you here for?" she asked.

I shrugged. "I'm one of the welcoming committees. I'm here for soldiers who don't have anyone to come home to. We give them a welcome home goody bag." I showed her the bags that had a bunch of different shit in it.

I'd been procuring little things from local businesses. Gift cards. Samples of their products. Fun stuff that wasn't related to a goddamn thing. Sometimes I went to Walmart or a drug store and filled the rest of the bag with candies and things that they couldn't get while deployed out of the country.

She smiled a warm smile. "That's so sweet!"

I guess.

But, when I'd started this particular chapter, it was due in part to Rafe.

He'd once said one of the hardest parts about coming home was that no one was here to care if they *were* home, or back in that hell hole, and my fifteen-year-old self had taken that to heart.

I'd worked with my stepmother, Shiloh, and had founded this chapter.

Ever since, I'd been attending every single welcoming home that I could possibly muster without taking time off from work or school. School that I was doing to humor my father.

Then the line of men getting off the plane shifted, and I caught sight of *him*. He was the last one off the plane. Literally, even the flight attendants had beat him off.

He was looking at the ground as he made his way down the long hallway that led to the open room where the family of the returning home soldiers waited. Even though his head was down, I knew for a fact that he was very much aware of the men and women ahead of him.

Butterflies swarmed my belly as I watched him prowl in my direction.

He hadn't seen me yet.

He wouldn't be happy to see me.

While he was still unaware of my existence, I watched him walk.

Watched the way he moved with purpose.

He was dressed in his military uniform.

Brown, darker brown, and tan digital camouflage head-to-toe. He even had a hat that matched his pants. The top shirt was open and flapping as he walked, showing off the skintight tan t-shirt he wore underneath. Was that part of his uniform? I didn't know. Then again, I didn't really care.

And boy, those pants.

His pockets looked like they were filled to the absolute brim with shit—and I wanted to know what he put in those pockets. Food? Socks? Guns?

Then there was that arm that was up by his neck that was latched on to the massive canvas bag that was slung over his shoulder. The veins in his tanned arm were thick and prominent, and I licked my lips.

He looked so unbelievably hot.

The pants he had on were tight. Not so tight that they hindered his movements, but tight enough that I could see his hips and thighs. I also noticed that he was wearing boxer briefs—mostly because I could see the seam around mid-thigh.

The shirt he was wearing was tight, too. His chest muscles bulged, and I vaguely wondered whether or not he had to go one size bigger due to the girth.

He abruptly turned left into the coffee house that was at the end of the escalator.

I looked over at Kayla, my best friend in the entire world.

She rolled her eyes and waved me away, causing me to grin at her.

"You're the best wingman ever."

"Or the stupidest," she commented as I raced toward the coffee place.

When I arrived, it was to find him with his back to the door, and his head tilted up so he could read the coffee menu.

I crept up in line behind him, wondering if he'd notice me.

He didn't—or at least he didn't act like he did.

The line crept forward, one-by-one, causing us to get closer and closer to the barista until finally we were there.

I shifted slightly to the side, causing him to glance at me.

He glanced away almost as fast, and I breathed a sigh of relief.

He didn't notice me.

Not in what I was wearing, anyway.

Then there was the fact that I'd dyed my hair purple and pink.

I also went lighter on the makeup nowadays than I did when I was younger.

His eyes were trained on the woman at the counter.

And not in a good way.

"I'll have a coffee. Large. Black." He paused. "And one of those blueberry muffins."

"I can't serve you. It's against company policy to serve anyone with a weapon." She eyed the bulge in Rafe's pockets. And, from the perspective at which I was standing, I could now see that that bulge was actually a hat and a cell phone. "Especially a military man like you," she said, sounding put out that she was having to have this conversation. "I mean, you kill innocent people. You don't deserve to walk this earth, let alone drink any coffee that I make."

Rafe blinked at the barista's words. Then shrugged and started to back away.

I placed my hand on his shoulder and stilled him. "Hold on a moment."

In fact, I'd said it with so much disdain that I was taken aback for a second.

A second.

"Hold on," I said more forcefully when he went to leave again.

That's when I realized he knew exactly who I was.

And maybe had known the entire time.

I winked at him and walked up to the counter. "I'll have a black coffee, large. Oh, and a blueberry muffin."

The barista's eyes furrowed, but she went to make the order, handing it to me a moment later.

I turned around and handed them to Rafe, and then offered the lady my card.

The lady glared at me.

I smiled, then narrowed my eyes.

Before she knew what was happening, I was at the counter and in the stupid bitch's face.

"Do you have any idea what this man has done to ensure that you can say stupid shit like you just said?"

The barista leaned back in affront. "Excuse me?"

"You heard me, lady. How could you speak to him like that?" I hissed. "You don't know him, or what he's been through. He asked for something to drink, not your goddamn liver."

"Excuse me?" the barista repeated.

Was that all the stupid girl could think up to say?

"Give him his freakin' drink if he ever comes around again. Now, I'd like an amaretto latte," I ground out, but stopped when the barista carefully reached for a cup. "No. Not you. Her."

The 'her' was actually a woman behind the bar that was counting the money. She looked like the manager or something and looked like she would rather not get into this argument.

"I'm sorry, but I'm counting the till. I can't stop until I'm done."

I narrowed my eyes. "I'll wait."

That's when I felt Rafe's dark eyes on me, and I blushed.

I actually meant to hide this entire time and not let him see me.

Why? Because when Rafe saw me, he left. Literally, he saw me coming, and he'd turn the other way. He'd avoided me for seven years like that, and I was beginning to think that it was something about me that he didn't like.

"Uh, hi." I waved. "How are you?"

I would've slapped myself on the forehead had he not been watching me with those blank, nearly black eyes.

"Fine," he answered, sounding so good that it physically hurt my heart.

I swallowed. "Are you going to drink that coffee?"

He shook his head.

I sighed and turned, seeing both women watching us.

"Your boss will be hearing about this," I informed them both, slapping down a ten. "I'd possibly start looking for another job."

The manager sneered. "You can try."

Oh, I *would* try.

Even if I had to plant evidence on that bitch's computer saying that she'd been stealing.

I didn't fight fair when it came to the ones I cared about.

I wasn't playing around.

Not when it came to how somebody treated a soldier.

I turned on my heels, still fuming, and froze.

Because Rafe wasn't there anymore.

He was just gone.

My heart sank, and my eyes started to burn.

He'd left.

I took a deep breath and blew it out, then returned to where I'd left Kayla.

I found her gathering up what was left of our signs, and then stowing them in a black trash bag that we'd use for the next time we came and did this.

"You almost ready?" I asked.

Kayla looked up, glanced around, and tilted her head. "No Rafe?"

I shook my head. "No Rafe."

She frowned. "Usually you don't get made that fast."

I started to laugh. "The barista at the coffee shop was a total bitch. I had to have a few words with her and ended up exposing myself."

Kayla just shook her head. "Ready?"

I nodded and we both started out, her holding the trash bag of signs, and me holding my purse and Kayla's.

Luckily the box with the goody bags was empty, meaning we weren't struggling like we were when we'd come in here earlier in the day.

"Did you see the woman have to be carted off by her husband earlier?" Kayla asked as we started into the parking lot.

"No, what happened?" I questioned, digging in Kayla's purse for my keys.

"You're in my purse, dummy," Kayla sighed.

I grunted and switched purses, coming up with my keys as I listened to Kayla explain what had happened.

"The woman was apparently in labor for like, five hours. But she wanted to meet her husband who was coming home from an eight-month deployment, so she just ignored them. When her husband showed, they kissed and smiled and laughed, and then her water broke all over his combat boots.

Gross.

"I was standing next to her earlier," I admitted. "I'm glad that she didn't do that to me. I'd have started crying."

I looked down at my flip-flop clad feet and grinned.

I didn't wear shoes anywhere if I could help it.

Then again, if I could help it, I didn't even leave the house.

Sometimes there were periods that I went two entire weeks without leaving.

It got to the point where I hired a lady to come clean my house—who also cleaned some of the other houses in the Free compound—and to bring my groceries.

Seriously, not a day went by that I had any regrets about being the homebody that I was.

"I saw you talking to her." Kayla laughed. "And you need to get over that aversion to bodily fluids. What are you going to do one day when some man has to spurt his load inside of you to get a baby?"

I literally shivered.

That'd been why I'd yet to go anywhere near a man and his penis.

A penis produced bodily fluid, and bodily fluids grossed me out.

Seriously, I might die a virgin.

"I'll deal with a man and his baby batter when the time comes, and not a moment…" I'd just passed the last car before mine and came to an abrupt stop. "…before."

"Baby batter?" Rafe asked, coming off of his slouch against my car. "I feel like I missed something."

He had. But we were not, under any circumstances, revisiting *that* conversation. So, he would forever be missing something.

"Hi, Rafe!" Kayla waved. "You glad to be home?"

Rafe turned his gaze from me to Kayla. "Yep."

He returned his eyes to me, and I could almost swear that he'd semi-smiled. It was there and gone so fast that I blinked, and then wasn't sure if I'd actually seen the phenomenon.

"Uhh," I said. "Do you want a ride?"

He nodded once. "Yeah, if you don't mind."

I nodded and gestured to my car. "You'll have to sit in the middle."

Rafe shook his head. "You sit in the middle, and I'll drive."

I thought about that for about point two seconds, then handed him my keys.

"You can't drive fast, though," I said worriedly. "My dad said that if I got another speeding ticket, he'd beat my ass and kick me off of his insurance."

Rafe's lips twitched. "Noted."

Kayla growled. "Can you open the trunk already, Janie? This shit is heavy."

I walked to the trunk and popped it open, then helped Kayla lay the signs in the back.

"Are you ever going to clean this out?" Kayla said in dismay.

I looked at all the stuff in the trunk and then shrugged. "Maybe."

In the back was about eighteen pairs of shoes, two that weren't even mine. They might've been my dad's. I didn't really know. I didn't have any male friends, but I thought they weren't too bad of an idea to have back there, so I left them.

Then there were the multiple sweatshirts, hunting jackets. A pair of waders that I'd used last duck season. A tent. A camp stove. Two propane lights. Groceries that I'd forgotten to get out of the car yesterday, and a hunting rifle.

"What's with the rifle?" Rafe asked.

I shrugged. "I had it to meet my dad at the range later."

Rafe grunted.

Kayla patted the signs and then walked around to the front seat.

"Why can't you get in the back?" Rafe asked.

I opened the door, and my puppies looked back at me with excitement.

"They're why."

"Why are they back there?" he asked.

I smiled and reached for Glock's head, giving him a good scratch behind the ears. Kimber pushed her nose out to sniff Rafe, but hesitated.

Rafe held his hand in a cup shape and extended it to Kimber, and I smiled.

So Rafe was a dog person.

Sweet.

"My babies failed K-9 training," I said. "There was this cop, his name is Trance. He had them for about a week and told me that these dogs were untrainable. That I'd already broken them."

Rafe started to laugh. "Any dog is trainable. You just have to find the right trainer."

"Well," I hesitated. "Trance brought them back on his way to visit with my dad and Uncle Sam. He said that all they would do for him was lay down. They didn't even perform for food." I sighed. "That's my fault, though. I turned them into lazy hounds."

I had two German Shepherd puppies that I'd gotten from Trance, and he'd said once they were a year old that I could bring them back if I wanted them trained—which I did.

But, apparently, allowing them to eat like humans meant that they didn't suffer being treated like actual dogs.

They were mad at me because Trance had kenneled them. They were mad that they no longer got fed actual meals—again, I was informed, that dogs should be eating dog food. Not people food. And, the icing on the cake, they'd both pouted like the spoiled rotten brats that they were the entire two weeks that they'd been gone.

Not only had it sucked for me that they were gone, but it'd also, apparently, sucked for them.

I'd been missing them like crazy these last two weeks, and honestly, I was happy to see that they'd felt the same way.

I'd gotten a call that Trance was dropping them by.

When I'd tried to let them in my place before I'd gone, they'd hauled ass for my car.

Once there, they'd climbed through the open window—the window that my father liked to lecture me about leaving down. Why, oh why, did I have to roll the window up when I was in the compound, under a freakin' carport?

The answer to that was: to keep your damn dogs from climbing into your car and refusing to leave.

Rafe gestured for me to get inside my car and then stepped back while holding the door.

I bit my lip and crawled in, very aware of how well my jeans fit my butt—and that was perfectly. I'd nearly had to apply butter to get these jeans on.

I may be young, but I was far from stupid.

I'd paid attention the few times that Rafe was around long enough for me to hold a conversation with him. I also knew that he preferred me in jeans.

How did I know that?

Because he'd paid more attention to me when I was fully clothed. I didn't know if it was due to the fact that I actually looked better in jeans or because he wasn't willing to look at me if I wasn't fully clothed.

Whatever the reason, I chose the route that would reveal the most of my assets, while still being modest enough that he would at least look at me and not look the other way.

So, I climbed in, tried to do it seductively, and then forgot to pay attention to the gear shift as I swung my knees around.

The minute the gear shift hit me in the knee, I started to whimper and fell over, straight into Kayla's lap.

"Oh my God!" I whined. "Kayla, kiss it and make it better!"

Kayla, being the dutiful, awesome best friend that she was, bent over and kissed it.

Then she smacked it.

"Bitch!" I cried. Literally cried. "Owwww, it fucking hurts. Jesus, it hurts worse than when I hit my funny bone!"

And I did that a lot.

Did I mention I was a klutz, too?

"Who is Trance?" Rafe questioned as he situated himself in the car while completely ignoring the fact that I was dying.

One could die from blunt force trauma to the knee, couldn't they?

Because I felt like I was.

"Trance is a member of the Dixie Wardens like Papa Silas," I wheezed. "The Benton, Louisiana Chapter. Not to be confused with the other nine million and thirteen chapters."

"Papa Silas?"

"Well," I hesitated. "He's Silas…but he's also kind of a grandfather. Even though he has a kid younger than me. But, still. He's Papa Silas to me. He told me Granddaddy Silas wasn't working for him."

"Actually," Kayla interrupted. "Janie has called him Papa for as long as we could remember. She tried to change it to Granddaddy Silas once when she was a kid and like she said, he told her no."

"Do you know who Silas is?" I questioned.

Everybody knew Silas.

And I could've sworn I'd seen Silas and Rafe in the same room as each other at least once over the years that Rafe had been around.

"Yeah," he said. "I also know Trance. Well, kind of. I know *who* he is, but I don't *know* him. Though, in the dog training world, he's pretty famous. Everyone knows the Spurlock dog training guru. I'm just surprised he couldn't whip your pups into shape. He's known for his perseverance."

I sighed. "That might've also been my fault," I admitted, my head still resting on the seat now next to Rafe's thigh.

"She told Trance to bring them home," Kayla said into the silence. "She called one night crying because she missed her 'friends.' She also asked to speak with them. Then, when they wouldn't talk, she told Trance to bring them home for a little visit. He brought them home mainly because he knew this wasn't going to work out. Janie treats them like her children. I'm also pretty convinced they'd kill me if I tried to take Janie anywhere without her permission. They already growl when I eat her food."

Rafe snorted.

"I taught them the things that were important. I can't have my extended family coming into my house and eating all my food. Food is expensive," I muttered, then sighed and sat up.

The children of Free really were awful. Justin, Elliott and Blaine's son, was the absolute worse.

"Sounds to me," Rafe said as he waited patiently for me to get situated. "That you didn't need to send them anywhere. If they already protect you, they most likely wouldn't need to be away from you at all. You just need to hone their already deeply ingrained instincts."

"How do you know all this?" I questioned, reaching for the seatbelt that would strap across my lap.

He stuck the key in the ignition and pressed the clutch with his left foot. His right hand came down on the gear shift. His forearm flexed as he dropped it into neutral.

I closed my eyes as I waited with bated breath for my car to roar to life, and seconds later, it did.

I shivered and opened my eyes, smiling widely.

"Janie's also insanely in love with her car," Kayla said with disgust in her voice. "You should feel privileged. She doesn't let anyone drive it, not even her dad."

That was true. I didn't let my dad drive it, though, because my dad wanted it.

My baby, my 1969 'Cuda, was my dream car. I'd found her on the side of the road outside of town. An old man had broken down there, and I'd offered him a lift to my dad's shop.

He'd looked haggard, beaten down and just plain sad.

The car, however, was pristine…at least on the inside. On the outside, she was a hunk of potential, but nowhere near the beauty she would one day become.

"Seems to me if your daddy bought you the car, you should at least let him drive it," Rafe drawled.

I won't punch him in the face. I won't punch him in the face.

"My daddy didn't buy me this car," I said. "I was given this car in a dilapidated state by a dying old man who was happy to find an owner for it who would love it as much as he did. My daddy and uncles helped me fix it up. The only thing they did, however, was the paint job. I didn't want to fuck it up with my lack of experience. So, they did that for me. The rest, though? That was all me."

"You know how to work on cars?"

Kayla started to snicker. "That's why she's always so dirty. I think you'll come to realize, my dear friend Rafe, that you shouldn't underestimate any of the girls in this family. Scout, Rebel, Janie, me, Sam's three girls. Hell, any of the Free girls, really. They all know their way around a vehicle. Janie here just knows her way better than most. She's the one who spent the most time with them."

Rafe looked at me, grinned, and put my baby into reverse.

His hand came perilously close to my left hip since I was half on Kayla's lap and half on the console, but he didn't touch me. Dammit.

"How fast do you think she'll go?" he questioned.

My car shook and shuttered, the car seemingly struggling to stay alive.

That was a lie, though. My car wouldn't die. This baby was perfectly primed and in the best shape a car of its age could ever be in. Hell, it was better than almost any new car I could drive off the lot.

"She'll go about one twenty and stay within the lines," I said almost instantly.

Kayla snorted.

Rafe didn't say a word.

But his hands did tighten slightly on the steering wheel, almost as if he was upset that I knew my car's top speed.

But…who didn't know their car's top speed? If you didn't, you were likely a wiener.

I, most definitely, wasn't a wiener.

"Where are you going?" I questioned as he expertly pulled out of the lot.

He didn't even stall. That was pretty impressive with my car.

I had a modified camshaft in it, and the proper fuel ratio made it persnickety sometimes. It took just the right amount of gas on the driver's part to get it to go without hesitating, and Rafe had applied it without ever being in it before.

That was damned impressive. My 'Cuda was a finicky little bitch.

"I'll go to your place. I have something I want to discuss with Sam anyway. Once I'm done, I gotta head to my sister's place. Then I have to head back down to Hostel," he answered, pulling out in front of a slow-moving minivan.

He went through the gears expertly, stopping in fourth gear and loosely letting his hand rest on the gear shift.

Glock and Kimber both woofed, causing me to snort. "Can you roll your window down for them?"

Rafe had it down moments later, and my hair started to fly all around my face.

"Their back windows don't go down?"

I shivered as the cool air hit my skin. "No. That's why I had this one and the other window cracked for them. The windows in the back need some work, and I haven't had the time to fix them since they stopped rolling down."

"Easy fix," Rafe muttered, his eyes going to the rearview mirror before he switched lanes.

He accelerated past a slow-moving dump truck, and then returned to his original lane.

"Maybe," I agreed. "What's in Hostel?"

"A job."

"What kind of job?" I questioned.

"One where I intend to work for a while," he answered, looking over at me for a short moment before returning his eyes to the road. "Why?"

I felt my lips turn up.

"Just figured that you had plans of some sort. Hostel's a small town," I admitted. "And I'm just curious."

"You're always curious," he muttered, sounding put out. "The road construction finished this way?"

I shook my head. "No, they hit a snag with a pipeline," I said as I gestured to a side road he should take. "That one is faster."

Rafe grunted but pulled off before the back road that I'd indicated. Instead, he'd taken some road that I'd never once seen before. A dirt road of some sort.

"Uhh," Kayla said. "I'm not sure this is a road."

"It is."

Then Rafe didn't say another word as we crawled carefully over the uneven road.

Minutes later, he pulled out onto the other side of the main highway again, right on the other side of traffic.

I'd lived in Kilgore my entire freakin' life and not once had I seen that road.

Otherwise, I would've taken it a whole lot more than just freakin' once.

"How did you find out about that cut through?" I questioned.

Rafe shrugged. "Research."

And that was the last word he'd said until we pulled into Free ten minutes later.

CHAPTER 2

*There are two kinds of people in this world. People with guns, like
me. And people with stupid, smug faces. Like you.*
-Rafe to Janie's ex

Rafe

I was going to die if I had to sit next to Janie another goddamn
second.

She smelled like sunshine and flowers, and I wanted nothing more
to haul her into my lap and devour her mouth.

But, a dirty old man like me couldn't be seen kissing the young
daughter of a friend.

Why?

Because I valued my last surviving ball, that's why.

Twelve years ago, I'd been shot in the upper thigh. That shot
hadn't taken out my ball. What it had taken out was the blood
supply to my testicles. Unfortunately, when blood supply was
restored, my favorite testicle was struggling. And, two days into
my recovery, it was discovered that my left testicle had given up
the ghost. Meaning, I'd gone back into surgery to have it removed.

I'd been asked at the time if I had any desire for a fake ball to be placed in my sac, but at the time, I hadn't given a fuck. That fuck had changed when I got my first good look at it after surgery—then I had to have it fixed. Swear to God, it looked awful, and the moment my prosthetic ball was in, I felt immensely better.

"Are you okay?" Janie asked, drawing me out of my ball contemplation.

"Fine," I answered. "Your parents change the gate code lately?"

Janie nodded. "Once a month like clockwork."

I sighed. "Are they going to make me jump through hopes to get it this time?"

Because, if I was an honest man, that really pissed me off.

I'd proven myself time and time again with them, and time and time again they made me prove myself all over again.

I should be used to it by now, but honestly, it was annoying.

I'd been loyal to them for over ten years now. I'd done everything they'd ever asked me to do, and yet they continued to treat me like the unknown. As if I was the man they always suspected me to be.

See, when I was a child—twelve or thirteen at most—my father had done something to a few people.

And one of those few people had been someone that the men of Free had known. An old Army captain of theirs that had just been starting out in life. One who'd invested in my father's Ponzi scheme and had lost his entire life savings—right when his wife was due to give birth to their first child.

From there, my father had just moved on to another unsuspecting soul. While Jerrod Teeterman, later known as Captain Teeterman, had struggled to keep up with what life had thrown him—which had been a wife who died shortly after giving birth to their very sick little boy. A very sick little boy who had struggled to live for four years before passing away when I'd just turned sixteen.

At sixteen, I hadn't realized that a man was losing his world a thousand miles away from me. What I had known was that in my own personal hell, life sucked. It was my sister and me, struggling to not get on my father's bad side.

If we got on that bad side? There would be hell to pay—there *was* hell to pay. I'd also found that out the hard way.

Lucky for me, after receiving the beating that put me in jeopardy of losing my life, my father had been taken into police custody.

It was then that they'd discovered not just the sins that had brought him under police scrutiny, but they also uncovered schemes he'd been a part of when his mug shot was plastered all over the news for his part in nearly beating me to death. They found over three hundred poor souls whom he'd cleaned out of their life savings and left floundering.

But life didn't get better after my father was in jail. Nope. Not for me, and certainly not for Raven, my baby sister.

How could it get worse?

Going from the devil that you knew to the one that you didn't.

Raven and I? We weren't strangers to bad situations. We'd spent years in fucked up situations.

After our mother's overdose, they'd placed Raven and I both in foster care. I had six months to realize that the life with the foster care family we'd been placed with was no better than the house we'd come from.

The judge that was the foster care father from hell was well known in the community. So well known, in fact, that he was always going to be believed over some delinquent boy insisting that something was wrong.

Raven had been subjected to the same treatment, but on a much smaller scale than me.

And the day that I turned eighteen, I tried to get her out. I'd made it to the next county over when I'd been pulled over by the sheriff of the county.

Then I was charged with kidnapping a minor.

After being thrown in jail on that bogus charge, Judge Paul Pearlman, the man who had ruined my life for the previous six months, informed me I had two choices. One, try to take my sister—his property—again and go to jail for some of the ugliest crimes I'd only ever heard about. Or, two, I could get the hell out and not come back.

He'd allowed me one concession: Raven's safety.

I'd held onto that promise as I packed my bags, and then walked out on my sister, not looking back as I became the newest soldier in the United States Army.

Life didn't get better after that.

Not even a little bit.

Raven thought I betrayed her and refused to talk to me. I was sure that Judge Pearlman fed her lie after lie.

What I didn't know was how bad it really was for her—something that I still wasn't sure I had the full story on.

Then there was the fact that my father's shenanigans hadn't just stopped at our small town. Nope. They'd extended into the military where he'd screwed over about fifteen different men just like Teeterman.

And, wouldn't you know it, but I somehow found myself with Drill Sargent Teeterman as my personal torturer throughout my first six weeks in the Army.

But, it didn't stop there.

Every step I took, I encountered another man my father had screwed over.

At one point, I'd thought about giving up. Especially when I was deployed the first time. Then the second. And the third.

When I was finally able to come home, I realized that things would never be better.

After being skipped over for promotion after promotion, screwed over, nearly killed, and basically treated like a piece of dog shit, I'd decided that was it.

I was getting out.

It'd been years of continuous torture.

The icing on the cake, however, had been when I was shot in the leg.

I'd found out that my doctor was yet another man who my father had screwed over.

I couldn't prove it, but it was just too damn convenient that he had the chance to fix what was wrong with my testicle and my leg, but conveniently didn't do his goddamn job?

No, I was far from stupid.

That was when I took the medical discharge that the US Army offered me and then found someone who would help me exact my own revenge.

From that day forward, I was just as involved in the Army—as well as the Navy, Marines and Air Force—as I was before I'd left it, but this time as a private consultant. One who worked with the military to uncover situations exactly like the one I'd been in during my four years in the Army.

Trace and me? We'd both been fucked over. We'd been treated like low lives—battered, bruised, hazed, fucked over and forced to do many things that we're not proud of today.

But, we'd gotten our men—and one woman.

We'd made the US military a better place to be, and in doing so, I'd found my calling in life.

Shortly after our first few years together, we'd branched out even farther into more global investigations, like the one that led me to Hostel.

After wrapping up the job overseas, I was heading straight to a town that was apparently the central hub of stolen military surplus.

But, while I was down there, I had a few other plans. Plans that centered around the fucking man who had purposefully held off on my surgery and nearly killed me in the process.

Over the years, I'd let go of a lot of my anger.

I'd taken Captain Teeterman's torture tactics. I'd taken the shit deployments. I'd done just about anything that was ever asked of me.

But, the one time that my life had been in danger for real, a certain

Army doc had played God with my life.

And he wasn't even discreet about it. He'd taunted me for years with it—he still taunted me with it.

I wanted him to know that I was there, and I was watching.

I also knew he had a daughter around Janie's age, and she was completely clueless to the fact that her father was a total piece of shit.

I was going to love uncovering the lies and deceit of Layton Trammel. I would also fucking love informing Elspeth Trammel that her father violated his medical oath to do no harm and purposely botched my surgery. And once I'd taken Trammel down, I'd be blowing that popsicle stand, hopefully never to look at that scum bag's face again.

"The code is 9191933," Janie said softly, pulling me out of my contemplation of how life was going to go for me for the next few months. "And all you have to do next time is text me, and I'll give you the code. My dad and uncles should know better."

I snorted. "Life doesn't work like that, Janie. Never has, never will."

Janie didn't have anything to say to that.

Twenty minutes later, when we parted ways—her going to her office, which was new, in the Free office building and me going to the conference room with Sam—I realized that Janie was still getting under my skin.

Only now, it was even worse than it once had been.

Staying away from her was going to be an impossible task.

Her ass in those jeans was the entire reason for it, too.

CHAPTER 3

People always look startled when you call them fuckface.
-T-shirt

Rafe

4 months later

Things were not always what they appeared to be.

"No fucking shit," I said to Trace. "This place? It's a goddamn smorgasbord of crime. And the person I thought was just another asshole in all of this is even more stupid than I originally thought. Apparently, the student has become the teacher."

This place was a complete clusterfuck. The cops in this town were corrupt. Shit was going on that even I didn't have the vein tapped on, which was saying something because not a thing went on around me that I didn't know about. It made me twitchy.

"What do you mean?" Trace asked warily.

"I mean that this entire fucking place is corrupt, and that dumbass, Layton Trammel, is at the epicenter of it all," I said, rubbing my eyes in a way that made my wariness known. "I haven't gotten anywhere near as much time devoted to this as I'd like with all the side jobs I'm doing, but I don't have a good feeling here. Something big is happening, and Trammel is right there in the thick of it."

"You need to drop the other jobs." Trace stated what I knew would come out of his mouth the minute I told him that I suspected a whole lot more was going on here than what we'd initially thought.

"No," I immediately declined. "They need me. I'm doing it; it'll just take me more time to get shit done. Which might be a good thing. If I'm seen around town more, I might be able to wiggle my way further into Trammel's operation.

Trace sighed. "Just don't let the other jobs get in the way of this one," he ordered.

I gave him a half-salute. "Yes, Daddy."

Trace flipped me off. "I'm not your daddy."

"No," I agreed. "Because you don't want to be my daddy."

Trace was older than me by about fifteen years, and I more than trusted his judgment on most matters.

As long as it wasn't matters of the heart, that was.

Trace had been through five wives. He has twelve kids with four of them and a child from a random hookup in another country during his first deployment.

He loved his kids…in his own way.

I think he saw them twice a year and talked to them about four times that on the phone. Then again, with twelve children, it was understandable that he'd not have as much time for them all as he would if he had a single child.

"So…Janie."

My eyes flicked up toward Trace and then shifted away. "We're not talking about her. Ever."

Trace started to laugh, not stopping even when I'd turned my back on him.

"Oh, come on!" He guffawed. "It's hilarious, and you know it. Admit it! You fell for a girl whose dad is going to kick your ass when you finally get in there."

"I'm not getting in there," I lied.

I was totally getting in there.

As soon as this job was done, anyway.

"You lie." He sat straight up and looked at me while rubbing his stomach. "And don't get too deep in this, man. Trust me on this. You won't like having to fight for her."

Trace would know. He'd had to fight for his current wife. The one who was 'the one.' Marci was a sweet lady, and she was like a mother hen, even to me, a man who was well into his forties.

Forty-one was in your forties, wasn't it?

I looked at my friend and sighed. "Back to Layton."

Trace's eyebrows rose.

"How does he not know who you are yet?"

I grinned. "Free did something good in the beginning. They let me know that my past wasn't buried quite as deep as I thought it was. They were only able to get a little bit on me, and I buried the rest of it so deep that I don't think even I can find it again. My previous name is solid, and with the recent additions in the form of the fuckedupness that is my face, Layton has no fuckin' clue who I am. Did I mention that he's looking to hitch his daughter?"

Trace snorted. "Don't marry the chick."

I *wouldn't* be marrying the chick. What I would be doing,
however, was getting in there so I could learn more about whatever
mess her father had gotten himself into. Then, when I had enough,
I'd blow this fucking town sky-fucking-high.

***

The meeting with Trace ran late, and by the time I arrived in
Kilgore to speak with the men of Free, they weren't happy with
me.

Six months ago, when they heard I was heading to Hostel, I was
tasked to do a little research, and what I'd found while I was down
there had been quite enlightening.

Now I was there to educate the men of Free with exactly what
they'd been sending their birds into, and I was not looking forward
to it. I just wanted to get this shit over with. Yesterday.

Which was why, when I arrived on my bike and tried to input the
code, I didn't bother trying to call anybody.

I did, however, climb the fuckin' fence.

It was ten feet tall and covered in razor wire at the top, but being
who I was, and what I did for a living, I'd learned to circumvent
that little deterrent a long time ago.

Arriving on the other side unscathed, I started walking up the main
lane, not surprised when a man came out of the garage—which
was in the front of the compound—moments later.

"You couldn't call?" Max, one of the men of Free, asked.

I shrugged.

"Could've." I muttered. "But I also wanted to fucking get this over
with, and not wait for one of you lazy assholes to let me in. I'm not

all that fond of waiting twenty minutes for one of y'all to decide I've waited long enough and take pity on me."

Max grinned. "How do you know we're not busy?"

I gestured to him. "You wouldn't have answered my breach as fast as you did if you were busy. I know damn well y'all always have someone monitoring. And you damn well know that at any given time, you have fifteen people here that can press a goddamn button and let me in."

Max shrugged. "Maybe we do, maybe we don't."

They did.

I knew what they had. I'd gone through it within a day of coming here the first time. Each house had access to the gate via a button, and most of them had at least two. They also had monitors that activated the moment that any movement was sensed.

So, no, I knew damn well that they all knew I was there. I also knew damn well that any of them could've let me in at any given goddamn time.

But, like I'd told him, I didn't have the time nor the inclination to wait while they made their fucking power plays.

I kept walking and Max fell into step beside me. A red rag appeared in his hand moments later as he wiped grease free from his hands.

"You're late," he said.

I shrugged. "Wreck on the interstate."

Which wasn't technically a lie. I just hadn't taken the interstate. I'd taken the back way, which also added five minutes to my commute. However, there were fewer people, which also meant my patience wouldn't be even thinner than it already was when I arrived for the meeting.

I knew I'd need to have all the patience I could muster when it came to dealing with these fuckers.

Then there was Janie.

"You suggested this meeting. Is it bad?"

"Yeah."

There was no reason to beat around the bush.

"Fuck," Max hissed. "Knew it."

I didn't make meetings with these fuckers unless I had to. I usually tried to spend time with people who generally liked me as a person. These men…they didn't.

They tolerated me, which was more than enough for the business we had together.

We remained silent the rest of the walk to the epicenter of the compound, which was where all their offices were held, as well as conference rooms, barracks for refugees, and the one thing that my heart wanted more than anything else.

Her.

Janie.

Speaking of the devil, she was running at us from another direction, her two dogs at her heels.

She was laughing, not paying attention to what was in front of her, and I swallowed at the joy that was written all over her face.

Or, it might've been the fucking pants she was wearing. If they could be called pants.

Really, they looked like fucking paint with how tight they were molded to her ass and thighs. And the billowy whatever-the-fuck-it-was that was supposed to be a shirt that she was wearing was thin as fuck, too. I could see her bra through it. Barely, but I could see it.

My dick started to harden, and I started to do multiplication tables in my head. When those didn't work, I started to take the square root of the numbers that I multiplied.

And yes, before you say, "That's not possible!" It was for me.

I was a certified genius. I could calculate things in my brain that people could barely enter into their calculator. I could also see things differently than anyone else. Understand things that baffled most people.

Everything came easily to me. Everything, that was, but relationships of any kind. Emotional. Physical. It didn't matter. I always managed to fuck them up.

But show me a computer, and I could crack it open and access anything and everything in less time than it took most people to take a piss.

If I didn't know something, all I had to do was read about it.

Did I also mention that I had a photographic memory?

Came in real handy when I needed to learn how to do something, that's for sure.

"Look who's decided to come out of her Bat Cave," Max drawled.

Janie looked up, smiled, and then froze when she saw me.

"Rafe, where's your bike?" she questioned.

I pointed with my thumb behind me. "Back there. At the gate."

She frowned. "I gave you my number. I also told you to call me if you needed in. I would've pressed the button on the wall that was literally two inches away from my hand."

I looked over at Max, who had the decency to look chagrined. "I didn't deny it."

No, he hadn't.

Fucker.

"I don't have your phone number programmed in my phone," I said.

Why didn't I have her phone number? Photographic memory, remember?

I also didn't have *anything* in my phone. Not a single saved number. Not a picture. Not an app that wasn't of use to me. Not anything.

"You don't need her phone number anyway. You want in, you call us," Max muttered low enough so only I could hear.

I would've rolled my eyes had I not known that he was completely, one hundred percent, serious.

He didn't want me anywhere around Janie.

They weren't stupid.

Janie was a beautiful woman—and she *was* a woman. Her hips, breasts, thighs, and ass all attested to that fact.

Luscious. Round. Beautiful.

God, she was breathtaking.

I wanted to…

"Rafe?"

I blinked, then looked up at her. "Yeah?"

"Max said to wait out here for a minute. Apparently, they have a woman inside that's deathly afraid of men," she repeated. "Shiloh is in there getting her moved to the safe room."

The safe room wasn't a typical 'safe room' as much as it was a room that the women could go to and feel safe. It didn't have anything special about it other than the women could input a code to get in, and not anyone—not even the men that owned the place—had the code.

It was more of a 'security' blanket than anything.

And I could probably break into that room in less than ten seconds if I really wanted to. Then again, so could the other men of Free.

But the women that came here didn't really know that. They just needed that security blanket for their peace of mind. What they didn't know, wouldn't hurt them.

"Oh," I muttered, then looked down at Janie's dogs instead of looking at Janie.

Because when I looked at Janie, I saw things that I shouldn't be seeing.

Such as her body underneath mine while I pumped away inside of her, spilling my seed and filling her womb with it—that kind of thing.

My eyes narrowed in on the dog sitting at Janie's side. The other one was sitting next to me, almost leaning into me, but not quite.

"Which one is next to you?" I asked.

"Glock," she answered. "Glock has the black mask. Kimber," she indicated the dog at my side. "Has more of a brown one."

I nodded, my eyes going to the dog at my side.

"Do they know basic commands?" I questioned.

"They do," she confirmed. "Sit, lay down, leave it, and paw."

"Hmmm," I murmured. "Have you tried teaching them anything else?"

She shook her head. "I watched a YouTube video once to try to learn how to do it, but every time I tried it with the two of them, they gave me this blank-eyed doggy stare that clearly said they had better things to be doing besides listening to me."

I snorted. "You have to give them some sort of incentive."

And that was how, for the next fifteen minutes while we waited to be given the all clear, I showed Janie how to do something small, but effective, with her dogs.

"How did you do that?" she whispered from my side, staring in awe as the dogs 'stayed.'

"Gotta find what they want, and that's your attention," I explained. "For some dogs, treats work fine, but other dogs are more stubborn. They would much rather have your excitement and assurances that they did good than a tiny partially-satisfying treat."

I backed away another pace from the two beautiful pups and then winked at Janie.

"Where did you learn to do this?" she pushed.

I whistled, and both dogs came instantly.

Janie bent down and rubbed each pup in turn, showering them with praises and excitement.

I tried not to be jealous of the damn dogs, but I didn't quite accomplish that feat.

The way she rubbed them all, allowing them to lick her face…yeah, I wanted to do that.

I was a grown ass man…and yet my body was acting like it was sixteen again instead of forty-fucking-one.

Seriously…I was a total freakin' goner.

Every single time I left and came back, it was like she got infinitely more beautiful.

And I thought six months ago when I saw her at the airport she'd been beautiful. Now? Well, now she was fuckin' gorgeous.

Dressed in her tight ass pants, loose white shirt, and simple pale pink Converse sneakers?

She didn't look special. She wasn't dressed up, and she sure as hell wasn't trying to impress anybody.

Which only served to impress me all the more.

It was her semi see-through shirt, that barely revealed a light green sports bra, that was really doing it for me, though.

She looked like everything I'd ever dreamed of.

"All right." The door finally opened, this time emitting Shiloh. "Y'all can go in now."

I grinned at Shiloh, James' wife, and winked. "How are you doing today, darlin'?"

Shiloh shook her head. "You and that sweet talkin' mouth aren't going to have any effect on me today. Janie, remember that you're picking Scout up from school, okay?"

Janie gave Shiloh a thumb up. "Will do."

Shiloh waved and she was gone, leaving us alone once again.

"I thought she was going to leave this place to the men?"

Janie snorted. "They all say that but then a woman comes in with a cute baby they can snuggle, and they all forget about their promises to stay away."

"I hear babies do that to women." I chuckled dryly.

"Not to me." She shivered like someone had just walked over her grave.

Which intrigued me. Didn't every woman want children?

"You say that like you don't want kids," I observed.

"I don't," she admitted. "At least, not anytime soon. I reserve the right to change my mind in the future, but right now, the thought of having kids gives me hives."

I snorted.

"You're young yet," I agreed. "Give it a couple years, though. You'll change your mind."

"It's not likely to change. I may be young, but I know what I want." she grunted.

The reminder of her age was enough to cause my dick to harden.

I didn't know what it was about her being that much younger than me, but every single time I thought about our age gap—at least since she'd turned a legal age of consent—I'd done nothing but think about having her.

I'd stayed away for so long that it was almost out of habit now, but each time I came back, it got harder and harder to deny.

I wanted her.

Badly.

And I wanted her bad enough that I didn't care what happened later on—namely what her father and her uncles would do to me if they ever caught on to my attraction.

Because, although everyone knew—even me since I'd seen her shoot—she could protect herself, that didn't mean that they weren't overly protective of her.

Hell, for the first five years I'd known them, they'd kept everyone away from me—women and children included.

It'd only been lately that I'd started seeing Janie more often.

She'd made herself an integral part of their operation with her computer skills.

Computer skills that I knew she used to check into me—but consistently came up empty each time she tried to dig deeper.

I think I was beginning to frustrate her, though, because she'd been doing it more and more lately.

"Rafe?"

Shit.

I hurried to the door that she was holding open and took it from her grasp. "Thanks."

"You're welcome," she said softly, then gasped when her dog cut her off, causing her to jerk backward and to the side.

I caught her before she could hit the wall and pulled her into my chest.

It was only for a few long seconds, but having her body pressed against mine had made my world shift on its axis.

I felt everything in the thirty seconds that she was pressed to me.

Her heart pounding in her chest. Her breasts pillowed on top of my arm. Her ass pressed against my dick—my very hard dick that stayed hard whenever she was in the vicinity. Her hair brushed my neck and face, and her hand automatically went to my arm to help keep herself from falling.

She gasped and turned, then smiled.

And I realized that I was fucking gone.

Absolutely and completely gone.

She owned me.

But then her father's voice coming from the conference room made me come to my senses, and I set her away from me.

"Gotta work on that with them, too. Personal space is important when it comes to dogs like that. You want them to protect you, not trip you up," I told her, acting for all I was worth as if I wasn't affected by her proximity.

Janie licked her lips. "Yeah."

"Yo!" Gabe yelled out. "We have shit to do today, Uniball! Let's get a move on!"

I growled.

Janie frowned.

And then I went into a meeting and told them what had occurred.

All the while I tried not to keep my eyes trained on the one thing in the room that was vying for my attention.

"You're telling me this motherfucker repossessed her car," Sam leaned forward in his seat.

"Shit." Janie hissed. "We discussed that we were going to pay off those car payments, but it never happened. Goddammit."

"Janie…"

Janie rolled her eyes at her father's quiet admonishment.

"Dad."

I would've snorted, but it would've brought attention to me, and I liked watching Janie without the men in the room being aware of my obsession.

"Tell us the rest," Sam muttered.

"Little Harold has his fat fingers in the cookie jar, and up his own ass. Skimming from the top, and from the bottom," I continued. "Impounds their cars, loses payments. Then he collects the late fees and keeps the cycle on repeat. Your newest bird down there got herself turned around but was so scared to say something and ruin what she had, that she took it for way too long."

There'd been another 'bird' there before this one, and she left rather abruptly. We'd received some independent reports that we had a problem down there. Not knowing what the exact problem was with Lark, one of their girls that was just relocated down there and not wanting to send another 'bird' to that area without knowing what that problem may be, he'd hired me. Reluctantly, but he'd hired me.

And, since it worked with everything else I already had going on down there, I agreed to take the job.

What I didn't expect was what I actually found, which I relayed to them.

"The bird has protection, though," I admitted. "She found a man there who will protect her—is already very protective of her—but Harold still needs to go."

Sam pinched the bridge of his nose. "I need another point of contact there then," he admitted. "Once we see if it's still safe, we'll find someone new as a point of contact down there."

"I have a suggestion," I started.

"Oh, this should be good, Uniball," Max muttered.

"It will be," Gabe snorted.

I sighed, then stood up.

"If y'all are done, I'm ready to go," I said. "I had to take time off to do this, and I don't have time to play y'all's stupid games today."

"Temper, temper," Jack muttered. "Tell us who you think will be good."

I started heading toward the door.

"The bird's new man."

Then I walked out without another word.

Or tried to, anyway.

I made it about halfway down the driveway before my name was called, and I was stopped by a hesitant voice that made my heart race.

"Rafe?"

I put one foot in front of the other again.

Bad.

Bad, bad, bad.

Don't do it, Rafe.

Don't do it, Rafe.

I lectured myself for the two minutes it took me to make my way down the driveway and hit the 'exit' button.

I slipped through the barely cracked open gate and then felt her hand on my shoulder.

I halted beside my bike and turned, trying not to betray the way she made me feel by being this close to me.

"Yeah?"

My voice didn't just fucking squeak, did it?

She'd been absolutely killing me during that meeting, and it'd taken everything I had in me not to betray the way I felt. The way I wanted to throw her onto any available surface and suck her fucking soul straight out of her pussy with my mouth.

"I'm sorry that my father and uncles say the stuff they say to you," she apologized. "Swear to God, they have more manners than that. I hope they didn't hurt your feelings."

I snorted. If I pussied out every single time someone called me a bad name, I'd be dead and gone a long fucking time ago.

"Your father can't hurt my feelings," I said. "Everything he's had to say so far isn't anything I haven't heard before."

Janie's eyes narrowed. "You hear this all the time?"

I laughed at that. "Honey, I'm the son of a man who screwed over military families, took their life savings, and left them desolate. I'm known far and wide. I might not have been the man behind the schemes, but I was the boy who was benefiting from their money. Military men have long memories, so believe me when I say, anything your family says to me, I've heard worse."

She frowned. "Rafe, just because you're used to it, doesn't make what they're saying to you all right. You should say something."

"I'm not going to say *anything*," I laughed.

Janie narrowed her eyes and pursed her lips, and I couldn't help but to allow my eyes to go to her mouth. That succulent, beautiful mouth with her pretty, puffy lips.

They were shining today with a sheen of lip gloss, and my hand twitched. It ached to wrap around her wrist, yank her to me, and lick those lips until they didn't shine anymore.

Goddammit.

My eyes moved away, and I found my eyes tuning into Janie's dogs.

"Your dogs are trying to dig under the fence," I muttered.

Janie turned and ran forward, bending down to the dogs' level to scold them.

She had her finger pointed at Glock's nose, and she was lecturing him on why he shouldn't do that, but all I could fucking look at was her ass in those pants.

I found my feet moving forward despite my brain screaming at me to stop.

I walked up until the large pillar hid my body from view and said, "Do you think that's going to help?"

Janie screeched and whirled, losing her balance.

I caught her before she could so much as tip slightly to the side.

And that was how I finally lost control.

Feeling her body pressed against mine, having those soft curves pressed against my sharp angles...I lost it.

My mouth found hers, and suddenly I lost the ability to make rational decisions.

My tongue moved out the moment our lips met and licked at the gloss. Apple. Her lips tasted like goddamn apple.

My. Fucking. Favorite.

I had a thing for apple.

It was my weakness.

The actual fruit. Apple muffins. Apple Cake. Apple ice cream.

Anything apple would do. I didn't discriminate against anything apple.

And Janie's lips tasting like my favorite thing in the world?

That was what caused me to do things I would've never normally done—at least that was what I kept telling myself.

My hands went up to her lower back, and I pulled her even tighter against me.

I'd never, not once in my life, lost control like I had in that moment.

I backed her up until she was pressed against the large stone pillar and plastered my body to her from chest to knees.

Janie's hands went to the fabric of my shirt and fisted, pulling me impossibly tighter.

My tongue tangled with hers, and I was so fucking turned on that I knew, had what happened next not happened, I would've taken her right then and there.

"Janie?" Sam called out. "Your fucking dogs better not be digging a hole in my wife's goddamn flower beds, or I'll never hear the end of it!"

I pushed off with a snarl and stared at Janie.

She stared right back, wide-eyed, mouth swollen from my kiss.

Her chest was heaving, and I nearly fucking came at the sight of her so disheveled.

Then, without another word, I turned my back on her—which was the hardest thing I'd ever had to do—and went to my bike.

I didn't look at her again as I started it and walked it backward out of the driveway.

Why?

Because I knew if I did, I'd be making the same mistake again, but this time, I wouldn't be stopping no matter who or what interrupted.

CHAPTER 4

I hate when people say Facebook is just for attention whores.
Sometimes it's for regular whores, too.
-Text from Janie to Kayla

Janie

1 month later

"Are you sure this'll work?" Kayla asked me for the fifteenth time.

"I'm going to hell," I moaned. "I really am, but I don't know what else to do!"

"Well this isn't the brightest thing you've ever done, that's for sure," Kayla muttered.

I threw my old panties at her, and she jumped away from them like an acrobat would when she tried to reach someone's hands on the set of rings across from her.

"Stop!" she cried. "That's so nasty!"

I stuck my tongue out at her.

"It's not nasty. They're only about an hour into my wear, they're still pretty fresh," I teased.

I'd be more inclined to agree with her if I'd worn them all day.

"This is beyond ridiculous," Kayla sighed. "You can't just go down there and expect him to let you in his door."

My brows rose. "I can't?"

"Janie, this is a bad idea."

I sighed. "Kayla, this isn't a bad idea. I have to try. I have to. If he won't let me stay with him, I'll just get a hotel room."

"Are you taking your dogs?"

I looked at Kayla and grinned.

"No." She immediately started to refuse. "No, no, no."

"Kayla," I drawled. "Pleasssse?"

Kayla growled. "If they wake me up in the morning just because they want something to eat, I will seriously fuck you up. I will call you, and maybe even call your dad, and scream at you both."

"Why my dad?"

"Because he refused to keep your dogs for you after that last time," she explained.

That was true. The last time I'd gone out of town, I'd had my dad watch the dogs. That had turned into a disaster because my dogs decided to howl all night because my father had locked them in the laundry room.

The only problem with that was my dogs like to roam all night long. They do what they want, and I let them because I'm such a sound sleeper.

My dad, however, was not. He woke up to the sound of their claws clicking on the floor and knew from having them over before that they were night owls.

And so, my dad had ignored the howls from the laundry room—or tried to anyway. When he'd gotten up the next morning, it was to find his entire room trashed. The drywall had been gouged. The hoses and cords from the washer and dryer were torn to pieces, and baskets of clothes shredded.

Yeah, it hadn't been good.

And now he refused to watch them.

Hence the reason I was asking my best friend to do it.

"I'm watching them at your house," Kayla said. "They're not coming to mine."

I snorted. "That's fine."

It wasn't like Kayla didn't live at my house half the time anyway.

We were best friends. Either she was at my place, or I was at hers.

Though, we were literally right next to each other.

Kayla's father, Dougie, had been a part of my father's unit when they were in the Army. He'd died while overseas when Kayla was a young child, and ever since, she'd been a pseudo-family member. My sister, though not by blood.

"Fine." She sighed. "But I'm only doing it until Monday. I have to be at an orientation in Benton, Louisiana on Tuesday. I want to leave on Monday so I'm not late for work on Tuesday."

I rolled my eyes.

Kayla was shadowing an officer named Bryce Rector, better known as Loki. He was a member of my grandfather's MC, and my grandfather had also been paramount in setting up this shadowing with the officer in the first place.

For some reason, Kayla wanted to be a police officer. However, Kayla also wanted to be a school teacher.

She was two years into both degrees and still wasn't sure what path she was taking.

Which was where my grandfather came in. Papa Silas had asked Loki if he'd be willing to let Kayla follow him around for a week or two so she could see what the job entailed. Loki had agreed, and now Kayla was going to be gone for two weeks while she learned the ins and outs of being a police officer.

Though my father had told her she could follow him around, we all knew that wasn't going to work. That would be because my father was just as protective of Kayla as he was about me. Meaning my father wouldn't let her really dig her heels in and see what it actually took to be a police officer.

Which was where my grandfather came in.

Silas was going to be watching over her, but Kayla would also get the real experience that she wouldn't be able to get here thanks to my father.

"I'll be back. Promise!" I held up my pinky finger.

Kayla sighed, took my finger in hers, and then we shook on it.

"Don't do anything stupid," Kayla drawled.

"Me?" I squeaked, batting my eyelashes. "Never!"

CHAPTER 5

I don't know why people complain about my appearance. My attitude is a lot worse.
-Rafe to Janie

Rafe

The last thing on my mind when I got home was entertaining.

However, when I pulled up in my driveway, drenched from head to toe in my own sweat, I found that my driveway wasn't empty like it usually was.

It was filled with cars.

Well, two of them, anyway.

I pulled my bike up to the carport door and shut it off before swinging my foot over the side of it.

The moment I was standing, I turned to find Elspeth, Layton Trammel's daughter, standing there with a warm, welcoming smile.

My stomach knotted.

"Hey," I said, sounding welcoming when I felt anything but. "What's going on? Why are you here?"

Why are you here?

I snorted.

I knew why she was here.

Last night I'd 'accidentally' bumped into her at the bar in town, and I had mentioned moving out to the new place on Old Highway Five. Apparently, Elspeth hadn't forgotten.

And now she was bringing me a pie.

How fucking sweet.

"I thought I'd welcome you to the neighborhood." She smiled, holding out the pie.

I didn't bother to tell her that I'd lived here for a while now. Three months, to be exact. I wasn't exactly 'new.'

However, I needed her—or, more accurately, the in with her father she could provide. I needed to be able to get closer to Layton to find out what he was doing and to do that, I was going to have to get closer to Elspeth.

I looked down at the pie Elspeth handed me and nearly grimaced.

Pecan pie.

I hated pecans.

My father used to have a bowl of them in his office, and I used to go steal them when he wasn't around.

The pecan likely still tasted good to me, but the thought of fucking pecans, which reminded me of my father, just turned me off.

I'd never eat another one of them for the rest of my life—not without thinking of my father—and I tried to do that as little as possible.

"Thank you," I grinned. "I really appreciate it."

The door to my house opened, and my eyes flicked up to see Janie standing there.

I immediately cursed.

Janie had called, said she was in town and had also requested to stay at my place.

Since I was a glutton for punishment, I'd agreed.

Which led to now—two women I needed in very different ways here in the same place at the same time.

Two very different women—one who meant something to me and one who was a means to an end—both staring at me with an expectant look in their eyes.

"Uhh," I hesitated. "Janie, this is Elspeth. Elspeth, this is Janie."

"Nice to meet you," Janie grinned. "I'm sorry I didn't answer earlier. I was taking a shower."

Elspeth's eyes went to Janie, and her jaw went tight.

I would've laughed had I not been needing Elspeth's pull to get me in with her father.

"It's okay," she lied.

Janie's smile turned warm, and her eyes turned to me.

"I'll just leave you to chat…" she hesitated, then backed out of the doorway and slammed it shut.

I turned back to Elspeth, holding the pie slightly away from my body due to the smell that was making me slightly sick to my stomach.

"Thank you so much for bringing it over," I smiled my congenial smile, the one that came out when I was trying to make someone at ease.

Nobody ever got the real me. Not even my sister.

The real me needed to be protected, because he actually gave a fuck.

Rafe Luis was always protecting himself because when he didn't? It always backfired.

Raven, my sister, had been my rock when we were growing up.

Then, one day that relationship took a hit because I couldn't take her with me. She's held a grudge against me for a long time, and still to this day, we were working to get back to how we used to be.

Sure, she'd 'forgiven' me. But I say forgiven loosely because I still wasn't altogether positive that my sister actually had, or if she'd just pretended that she had.

Anyway, the smile that I gave Elspeth wouldn't have worked with Janie. She would've known that I was schmoozing, which was why I was glad that she'd gone back inside.

"Who is that *girl*?"

The way she said girl made the hair on the back of my neck stand on end.

"A friend." I smiled. "She's the daughter of one of the men I work with."

As far as anyone down here could tell, I was a crew member of Hail Auto Recovery, a towing company in Hostel, Texas.

As for the what the rest of the world knew of me? They didn't know what I did, which was the way I liked to keep it.

Janie included.

"Daughter," Elspeth hummed. "That's good to know."

Then she smiled a secret smile at me, and I felt my stomach clench. But not in appreciation, in worry. I hoped that Janie didn't see her because I did not want her to do or say anything to hurt my investigation. I'd done a lot of work insinuating myself into the perfect position to survey Layton Trammel, and I was not going to be happy if anything happened to jeopardize it. I wanted to go home, and I couldn't go home until I finished one final thing.

And once that one final thing was taken care of? I was going to go hide in my cabin for six months and not do a single damn thing.

At least, until Trace needed me.

This entire thing had been fucking exhausting.

When I'd arrived in Hostel, I hadn't realized what I would be walking into. I hadn't realized that one thing would come up after the other and that soon I'd be dealing with way more than I ever intended to.

I also hadn't intended to actually work on top of that.

So now, I was working a regular job with Hail Auto—when I had time, that was. I was working for Free, dealing with those issues, and I was working my own case. There were days that I was lucky if I got three or four hours of sleep, and I was fucking tired.

I needed a fucking break.

Yesterday.

"Anyway," Elspeth smiled. "I'll let you enjoy that pie and go.

Welcome to the neighborhood."

I smiled—my nice smile again—and waved.

The moment she turned around, I didn't hesitate to turn myself and head to my door.

I didn't bother watching her go, either.

She wasn't Janie, after all. She didn't have Janie's ass. She didn't have Janie's juicy thighs. She didn't have anything *Janie*.

I was so Fucked.

Fucked with a capital F.

I walked into my house, and the first thing I saw the moment the door opened was Janie's ass in the air, bent over my couch, as she tried to reach the remote control that had fallen on the floor.

It was well out of her reach, yet she stretched farther and farther until she was precariously close to falling completely over.

I swallowed and looked around the room, noticing all her things.

On my coffee table sat her old, raggedy looking shoes. Those stupid Converses were the cutest things I'd ever seen on her feet. I'd always hated Converse sneakers. Always. They were useless for anything but casual wearing. I couldn't go hiking in them because they didn't protect my feet from sharp rocks. I couldn't wear them in the rain since they didn't shield my feet from the wet. And wearing them in the cold? That was just plain stupid. They offered absolutely zero protection from that.

But on her? She pulled them off, and they didn't make me want to throw them away like they had when my sister had worn them.

Her computer—which had half a million stickers on it—sat on the couch next to her. What looked like code was pulled up on the screen, but without moving closer, I couldn't tell for sure due to the glare on the screen.

She was wearing a sweatshirt—which I might add was mine—that completely engulfed her small frame. Her shorts were so short that they were tucked up under the sweatshirt, making it look like she wasn't wearing anything at all.

And those goddamn toes of hers were painted neon green and highlighter-fucking-yellow. They alternated in a pattern, and they were so freakin' cute that I realized that I might very well be delusional.

What the hell was it about Janie that had me thinking everything about her was so fucking cute?

Because she is cute, dumbass.

My inner monologue wasn't appreciated at this moment in time, so I moved farther into the room and walked up to where Janie was still reaching for the remote.

Once within reach, I bent down, picked it up and then held it out to her.

She gasped, surprised to see me standing there, and growled.

"You scared the shit out of me!" she hissed, falling back on the couch and slapping her hand over her chest as if to help calm her heart.

"I wasn't quiet when I came inside," I pointed out. "What are you doing here?"

Janie grinned. "You know why I'm here."

"I know why you told me you were here," I countered. "But why are you really here?"

Because if she even hinted it was because of that kiss right now, I would rip that sweatshirt from her body, tie her to the chair with it, and then I'd fuck the absolute hell out of her.

Janie bit her lip, and I realized that I was going to have to go for it.

This thing between us was unreal, and it wasn't going away.

I'd have to fuck her.

Then, after I fucked her, maybe I could control myself.

Maybe what we had going on wasn't as explosive as I thought it was.

Maybe, just maybe, I was fucking crazy, and it was all some sort of irrational reaction.

Maybe we could get each other out of our systems.

"Because of the kiss."

And there it was.

I moved.

The pie moved with me and fell in my haste to get to her. It fell, catching the lip of the coffee table on its way down, scattering bits, globs and pieces everywhere.

It didn't matter. I'd clean it up later.

Or maybe I would bring the Shop Vac in here and suck it up.

Whatever. I didn't fucking care.

I lunged toward the couch, and Janie gasped in surprise.

She didn't hesitate when I lifted the sweatshirt from her body.

Her limp, wet hair fell against her skin of her back, causing her to shiver.

Let her be cold.

It'd only make her nipples harder.

"Stand up," I ordered.

Her chest was heaving, and her eyes were wide.

But she stood up.

I don't know if she sensed my instability or what, because she didn't make a move. She didn't so much as twitch her lips.

"Go to the coffee table and lay down," I rasped. "On your back."

She looked down at the coffee table where half of the pie was in a puddle, making a dripping mess as it spilled over the sides, but didn't so much as hesitate.

"Do you want my shorts off first?" she asked as she took a step.

I grinned—this grin was as fucking real as it got with me—and shook my head. "No."

She went to the coffee table and laid down, then spread her legs so that they were on either side of the table, her toes mere inches from the floor.

I walked to her and looked down at her.

"Don't move."

She licked her lips. "Yes, sir."

Something about her calling me sir felt so goddamn right that my dick hardened to full mast in my pants. If any more blood made its way to my engorged cock, it'd literally burst.

I reached into my pocket and pulled out my pocket knife. It was an Old Timer. Ugly and yellow.

I'd found it in the street when I was eleven, and I had carried it with me ever since.

I'd never once been more grateful that I'd decided to always have it with me than I was right then as I took the knife to Janie's shorts and cut them at the seams.

The shorts fell from her body as Janie's gasp filled the air.

"I could've taken them off for you," she whispered breathlessly.

I grinned. "Yeah, but then I couldn't have gotten the enjoyment out of cutting them from your body, now could I?"

She curled her lips over her teeth but didn't say a word.

I took the knife to her shirt next. Cutting it straight down the middle from collar to belly. I felt a brief moment of regret at cutting something off her body that molded so perfectly to her breasts.

However, once those breasts were exposed to me for the first time, my momentary flash of guilt fled.

She had the most perfect breasts I'd ever seen.

Perky with blush-colored nipples, I wanted to devour them.

They'd also bounce nicely when I started to thrust roughly inside of her.

Fuck. Me.

"What now?" she breathed.

I trailed the tip of the knife lightly down her chest, belly, and then pubic bone, coming to a stop once I reached the leg hole of her panties.

I hooked one single finger in the waistband, and then tugged the knife up, shredding one side of the lace.

The other leg hole followed, and I yanked the material out from under her, then brought it up to my nose.

Her eyes widened as I inhaled deeply, and her mouth parted.

"Smells like everything I've ever hoped for," I informed her, then shoved that scrap of fabric into the back pocket of my jeans.

She swallowed thickly as I took the knife and slammed it blade first into the wood next to her side. Once it stopped wobbling, I yanked her down until her legs hung over the coffee table completely, and her ass was at the edge, exactly where I wanted it to be.

Then, the harsh crack of my hand slapping against the side of her ass and hip had her jumping in surprise, momentarily distracting her long enough for me to do what I did next.

"Put your knees to your chest," I ordered.

The coffee table was the perfect size.

Small enough for her body to barely fit, but tall enough for me to be at the perfect height to do what I wanted to do.

She did as she was told, and I nearly went down on my knees when her pussy was exposed to me for the first time. Her legs went up and fell to the side, nearly touching the table with the front of her thighs with how wide she'd spread herself open.

So fucking flexible.

So sweet and pink, I wanted to lick it all up and never stop.

I picked up the sweatshirt from the floor and wrapped it around her body, as well as the coffee table, then wound the arms of the sweatshirt tightly around her lower half, tying her into that folded position with the front of her thighs touching the wood of the coffee table at her sides.

Once I had it tight enough, I moved the knot of the sweatshirt arms high up, just under the back of her knees, ensuring that the sweatshirt would stay in place if she decided to move.

Which she did in the next instant.

She rocked her hips, trying out the bonds, and her eyes widened when the fabric creaked—the knot only tightening.

She scowled, which caused me to grin.

"I think I forgot to mention I'm into bondage," I teased casually. "You really are in over your head, little girl."

She licked her lips in worry.

I could practically read the fear on her face.

"Afraid you agree that you're in over her head, girl?" I teased, running the tip of one finger down the inner seam of her thighs. Not quite touching her pussy, but not quite appropriate, either.

She shivered at the feel of my finger touching her delicate skin, and I didn't miss the speed in which her breathing had picked up.

But she didn't deny me.

She didn't pull away.

Didn't say no or tell me to go fuck myself.

She only looked at me with those goddamn mesmerizing eyes that were practically begging me to fuck her and fuck her hard.

Something I would be doing.

Soon.

But for now, I had two fantasies that needed to be fulfilled before I got my cock anywhere near her.

Because I knew, once my cock touched that perfect pussy of hers, I wouldn't take my time.

I wouldn't be gentle, and I wouldn't hesitate.

I'd fuck her and keep on fucking her until I couldn't fuck her anymore.

Until all the energy left my body and I was left a husk of a man.

I dropped down to my knees beside her and then leaned over to take a deep inhale of her pussy straight from the source this time.

She smelled divine.

Ripe and sweet, exactly like I'd always dreamed.

"Please," she breathed, trying to move her hips.

I smirked, then dropped forward until her pussy lips were inches from my face.

The moment that my tongue was close enough, I took one single swipe from clit to anus, and felt her flavor practically burst on my tongue.

I growled in surprise at her sweet taste and immediately went back for seconds.

Then thirds and fourths.

Until finally, I buried my face in her pussy and inhaled her.

Licking, sucking, and playing, I didn't stop until she was on the verge of orgasm.

But, the moment she got close, I pulled away, not willing to let her come yet.

"Please," Janie keened.

I brought my hand up and circled that tight bud with one finger.

The coffee table jolted with her jump of surprise.

I chuckled darkly, then moved that finger down to swirl around her entrance.

She shivered, her pussy clenching on empty air, searching for my finger as if she knew that I was going to insert it any moment.

But I wouldn't.

The first thing that was entering Janie's body would be my cock, not my fingers.

I wanted her to feel my cock for days after I had her, to remember that it was me who made her sting every time she moved.

I leaned over and snatched the fat pillow off the couch, then put it on the ground where I was kneeling.

Moments later I stood and started to strip.

She watched me with eyes glazed in passion, her mouth slightly open, and her nipples peaked.

I lost the shirt, first.

And her eyes took absolutely everything in. My chest. My six-pack. My V.

Oh, and my gun that was hiding one side of that V that I was carrying in an appendix carry.

Her eyes flicked back up to my eyes, and she took a deep breath, almost as if she was steeling herself for what was to come.

I winked.

She was a smart girl.

Janie shivered.

I removed the gun from my belt and placed it carefully on the table next to the couch, then moved to the belt of my pants.

I tossed it up by her head for later, just in case she got unruly and tried to do things with her hands—you know, like touch me and force me to lose the last bit of control that I was already desperately holding onto with everything I had.

My pants sagged the moment that my belt was gone, riding down low on my hips to expose the fact that I wasn't wearing underwear.

Which she noticed very quickly.

She took a deep breath, causing her chest to rise, and my eyes to go to those breasts that I hadn't had proper time to play with yet. But I would.

Soon.

Just not right now.

Right now, I had one thing on my mind, and that was sinking my cock inside of her until neither of us could tell where she ended, and I began.

Then, once I sufficiently reminded her of who she was messing with, I'd start the whole process all over again.

Whatever errand she was down here for was about to be put on hold, and I would be the one to put it there.

After unbuttoning and unzipping, my hands went to the waistband of my jeans, and I pushed them off my hips. They fell to my feet with what felt like the loudest whisper I'd ever heard.

Janie's gasp was enough to give me a fuckin' complex.

I knew what she saw.

I had a big dick, and I knew it.

I'd known it since I was a kid in high school and could compare.

But Janie's eyes went from lust to worry, and I grinned.

"Not sure you want to play anymore?" I teased, fisting my cock and giving it a pump.

She licked her lips and then croaked, "I've never wanted anything more in my life. I'm just wondering if I'll be able to walk afterward."

I dropped down onto the pillow, which lifted me to *just* the right height to place my cock directly at her entrance, then leaned forward to run the length of the underside along her wet cleft.

She gasped and arched, her breasts heaving, as my cock head touched her clit.

I grinned, then did it again. And again. And again.

I repeated the process until she was squirming, and my cock was fully coated in her excitement.

Then I notched the head at her entrance and slowly started to forge my way inside.

I didn't stop until I physically couldn't get any more inside of her without hurting her, and then started to pull back.

We repeated that process three more times before I was satisfied that she'd taken all of me that she could, then I stopped and studied her.

Her eyes were once again in the zone of euphoria, her breasts tightly peaked, and she had a flush rising over her chest.

Her mouth was closed, and her jaw was tight, but those eyes were aimed directly at me.

Wanting more.

"Ready?"

Janie smiled. "Oh, yeah."

I pulled back and slammed back inside, my ball sack hitting her anus as I did.

I kept my eyes on her tits at first, enjoying the show as they bounced and bobbled, knowing if I looked down at where Janie was split open, impaled on my dick, I would come.

She felt so warm, wet and tight.

Three of my favorite things in the entire freakin' world.

She also felt forbidden, like what I was doing was a bad thing.

Something that was going to blow up in my face.

Yet, I didn't stop.

Didn't second guess the feelings that she pulled out of me.

Only felt.

And, by only feeling, I'd worked myself up into a tizzy.

I was so focused on her tits as I fucked her pussy, I almost missed the warning signs.

However, when she started to come, I continued the pace, letting her ride it out.

See, that is where most men go wrong.

When she's on the verge of coming, you don't change anything that you're doing. Why? Because you're obviously doing something right, otherwise she wouldn't be coming.

See? Simple deductive reasoning.

But, by her coming, it made me lose focus on her breasts.

My eyes went to her pussy, which was flooded with her release, and I lost it myself.

The way she looked so full to bursting, flowering so beautifully around my cock, had my come boiling.

Her clit was raised and red, and I wanted it in my mouth so bad that I could almost taste it.

And that was when I started to come.

Inside of her.

Without a condom.

I filled her full of everything that I had to give, and I didn't stop until I was spent.

My eyes went up and met hers, and something was exchanged between us in that moment.

A moment of understanding, you could say.

This thing we had between us? It wasn't something that was going to go away.

Not now. Not ever.

Therefore, I needed to figure out a way to make her mine, without also ruining everything I had.

Everything she had.

Because I wouldn't do that to her.

Me? I had absolutely no problem changing everything for her.

But she actually had a family who cared about her and who she, in turn, cared for deeply.

I had nothing to lose, and she had everything.

CHAPTER 6

If you write fu*k instead of fuck, Jesus still knows. And he probably thinks you're a pussy like I do.
-Food for thought

Janie

Two weeks later

I should've known the moment he walked in the door that today was going to be a good day.

But, I'd already been having a really shitty day.

Why, you ask?

Because I missed him.

I missed him so much that I was practically begging my phone to ring.

Which it never did.

Never.

I should've known after I walked out of his door that it wouldn't end like I wanted it to end. That I'd go home, and not hear a single word from him since.

But, I was stupid, naïve, and wanted to think the best of everyone.

However, my excitement suddenly dimmed when Rafe walked through the door, followed moments later by a large blond male that reminded me of one of those men off of the TV show, *Vikings*, and a woman that was cute and leaning toward the man like he was her lifeline.

I looked at Rafe curiously.

He mouthed two words: Get Sam.

I did what he requested, unable to ignore his orders.

Why? Because I was a slut. A slut who was a glutton for punishment.

"Uncle Sam?"

Sam looked up from his desk. "Yeah, Janie?"

"Rafe's here with a couple," I murmured.

He frowned, then stood up.

I backed out of the room and went back to my own office where I was working on a report…a report that was probably going to take way longer to do now that Rafe was here.

God, I hadn't seen Rafe for a total of two weeks. That was fourteen days. Fourteen days, three hours, and twenty-nine minutes, to be exact. I should be mad that he hadn't returned my texts. I should be mad that he never came to follow up. I should be mad…but I wasn't.

Disappointed, yes. Mad, no.

I knew when I took my clothes off for him and laid on that coffee table that what I was about to do would likely only be a one-time deal.

Did it stop me from doing it? *Hell no.*

Would it stop me from doing it again? Again, *hell no.*

Uncle Sam said a few words to Rafe, then grunted something and went to Jack's office. Jack followed him out and went to the meeting room as Sam then went to Max's office.

Max limped out.

His knee must be acting up today.

I frowned.

"Did you take your medication?" I questioned him.

Max scowled at me. "No."

"The medication is an anti-inflammatory," I told him. "It'll help with the swelling, so it doesn't hurt so bad."

Max had just had knee surgery a few weeks ago, and he was doing exceptionally well. Though that likely had to do with the fact that he was in great shape for his age, and he worked his ass off to get back to where he was.

But, he was a stubborn ass, and he needed to take his meds.

I sat at my desk and pulled out my phone, texting Peyton, Max's wife, to tell on him, at the same time I started to eat the sandwich I'd made before all of the excitement started.

Grinning at the response I got in return, I put the phone back down and went back to my report.

And, the entire time the meeting was taking place, I kept my eyes on Rafe through the partially open door.

I couldn't help it.

I was trying not to make a fool of myself by throwing myself at him.

Then somebody cleared their throat, and I looked over to see my Uncle Sam frowning at me.

I flushed and went back to my report, but I couldn't help but listen to their discussion.

The man, Dante, and the woman, Cobie, were here because of another guy, Drake, who was doing some not so good things.

Those not so good things turned out to be Dante suspecting Drake of killing one of *our 'birds.'* They were also discussing a few other things, such as the suspicion of that same man killing their infant son.

A bird, if I could remember right, that had willingly gone back to her husband. A first for us.

I'd actually looked into that one myself and had been watching over her from afar.

Though, every time I'd tried to get in contact with her, she'd be extremely evasive.

But, I couldn't save her if she didn't want to be saved.

I immediately started to pull up my old files.

I'd looked into the man, as well as the woman.

On the surface, though, everything seemed legit.

But I still printed them out, because I knew it was only going to take a few minutes for one of them to ask for the report I had.

That request came moments later when my Uncle Sam came to the partially closed door and looked at me.

"Janie?"

I grinned and picked up my pickle in the opposite hand of my sandwich.

"Yeah?" I questioned as I leaned forward to take a bite of my pickle.

It crunched noisily, and I looked sheepishly around the room, pausing only slightly on Rafe a little longer than the others, before returning my gaze to Sam.

"Can you do me a favor and bring me the report on a Drake Garwood?" he asked me. "Everything."

I gave a chin tilt in answer and turned, not missing the way Rafe's eyes slid over every single inch of my body.

I shivered as I returned to my previous activities, finished my pickle, and pulled my report off the printer.

I tried not to listen to the discussion—Uncle Sam hated it when I got too much into the particulars of cases without him vetting my safety—but it was hard not to hear.

Especially when the topic of conversation changed from the man, Drake Garwood, and moved to the child of Drake Garwood and Marianne Garwood—our bird. The child had been killed, and everyone suspected that the father was behind it.

My ears tuned into the conversation they were having as I finished what was left of my sandwich.

I became so engrossed in my food that I forgot I was listening to the men and women speak in the other room.

What had enlightened me was the silence of the room beyond.

"Well," Jack muttered. "I haven't heard back from Winter yet. Once I do, I can give you the number on those boxes…do you mind if I keep this?"

I didn't bother to say that I could find that information out.

Mostly because, again, they didn't want me in the middle of a case that could possibly threaten my safety.

My father had made it clear the day I started to help them that under no circumstance was I allowed to do anything that could quite possibly put me in danger.

Therein lay my problem.

I was still being treated like a child at the age of twenty-three.

I was treated as though I couldn't possibly know as much as I did know, and if I even tried to get into a conversation I wasn't invited to, I was lectured non-stop.

Which was also why I hightailed it out of there when I did.

The look I got from Uncle Sam was one of anger. One that said if I stayed, I wouldn't like the consequences…kind of like I didn't like them last time.

See, my family was adamant that I wouldn't get caught up in the dangerous side of the family business—and that was pretty much all of it but printing off notes and making myself useful for coffee runs.

Sam didn't want my dad mad at him, and if that meant hurting my feelings, he'd do it.

What he would also do was give me the boot—which he'd

threatened before.

Hence the reason I left.

Without me there, he couldn't yell at me.

Maybe by the time he did find me, he might have calmed down.

I grimaced as I hurried out of the building, then hurried toward my place.

Once I collected my dogs, I further decided to leave altogether.

Choosing a walk over an angry lecture, I headed down the driveway without picking up my head so as not to make eye contact with anyone, thereby ensuring that I wouldn't have to talk to any of them, either. Because most of them would surely find out that I was upset, and that would be a longer conversation than I wanted to have at this moment in time.

The dogs stayed at my feet as I hurried out of the gate and took a left. Immediately my feet took me on my familiar trail, and I was walking partially shaded by the woods on the side of the road, easily hidden from approaching cars—or bikes.

At least, I thought I was.

And I was thinking I was alone, too, until I felt someone yank on my arm from a tree I'd just passed, causing me to gasp.

And then I felt myself being pressed against a familiar, hard chest.

Oh, and my dogs going absolutely wild.

"Call 'em off, honey," Rafe's velvety soft voice said in my ear.

I shivered, then turned and 'called them off.'

"Kimber and Glock, sit."

Both dogs sat, but they didn't look happy to be doing so.

"Good dogs," he said.

I blinked then turned.

"Yeah?"

He nodded. "They were aware I was here the entire time, trailing you. You should pay more attention to their cues, though. They can't talk, so you'll have to glance at them every once in a while. But, they didn't move or do anything until after I'd grabbed you. I'm guessing they knew I wasn't a threat, or at least they thought I wasn't. Then, they weren't so sure, so they started to bark."

I blinked.

"Well," I hesitated. "That's kind of awesome, isn't it?"

He winked. "You bet."

I frowned. "What are you doing here?"

He opened his mouth, then immediately closed it.

"Something I shouldn't be doin'," he finally settled on.

"And what would that be…" I questioned, my heart starting to pound. "Because I haven't the slightest idea."

And I really didn't.

He hadn't called. He hadn't texted. Hell, I hadn't even gotten a smoke signal—something I knew that he was likely more than capable of giving me.

I was literally sitting on my hands, waiting for something to happen.

Something I really, *really* wanted to happen.

I wanted him to make that move.

I wanted to do a lot of things more than what I'd done with him—such as actually hold a conversation that didn't have him running the other way when my family came into the room. Or involve us only talking with our bodies. Not that I was complaining about that last bit.

I could go for more of that.

In fact, the more I thought about how he felt pressed up against me, the more my mind continued to spiral out of control until I couldn't even hide what I was feeling anymore.

"Janie," Rafe growled.

I shivered at the sound of his voice.

"Yeah?" I licked my lips, staring into his eyes as I did.

Those eyes of his darkened impossibly further, and I swear I felt that straight to my soul.

"Don't look at me like that," he ordered.

I blew out a breath. "I don't know if I can help it."

He leaned forward so close that I felt his beard against my lips as he spoke. "I have so many things wrong right now that being here with you is the only thing right...but I can't do *that* with your father able to walk up on us at any moment."

I swallowed.

"What my father doesn't know won't hurt him," I informed my torturer.

"There are game trails all along this stretch of woods," he said softly, tucking a few stray hairs that'd escaped my messy bun behind my ear as he spoke. "Not to mention that they have live feed. I like you, darlin'. But I also like my face."

I grinned, and then took a step back. "Well, I can't be that close to you then."

He smiled, but that smile quickly fell.

"I have some things I'd like to discuss with you…but then that came up."

"What?" I questioned.

"That with Dante and Cobie. I've meant to call you for a while now, but my life…" he sighed. "My life is complicated. I don't have time to even go see my sister. I just don't want you to think that I forgot about you."

I swallowed, touched that he'd even take the time to say anything to me at all, let alone explain his actions.

Rafe didn't seem the type to explain.

He seemed the type to tell a person how it was, and then expect to be obeyed.

My hand rose, and my fingers started to curl around the stray hair he'd tucked behind my ear as I said, "I think I can wait for you to uncomplicate it."

His grin was bright.

And with a wink, he was gone, disappearing into the woods almost as fast as he'd appeared.

Unfortunately, I had no idea that by promising that, I'd be waiting far longer than I ever intended

Lani Lynn Vale

CHAPTER 7

I hate it when I say I hate everyone, and then the one person I hate the most laughs and says, 'not me, right?' No, bitch. I especially hate you.
-Conversation between Rafe to Janie

Rafe

Eight weeks later

Nobody ever prepares for a grenade.

Nobody.

Sure, you might think about how you'd react if a grenade was thrown in your direction, but until you've actually had a live one thrown at you without warning, you have no fuckin' clue how you'll react.

There I was, texting Trace about my new "friend" Layton Trammell and his daughter, who wouldn't leave me the fuck alone no matter how hard I tried to avoid her, while simultaneously watching over Cobie and Dante's daughter, Mary, when it happened.

The entire room exploded.

My ears rang.

My body was thrown backward, and somewhere in the confusion, I was able to right myself.

The lights were too bright, and the air around me had a funny smell to it.

I couldn't quite focus, and I was fairly sure that my head was fucked up.

I couldn't feel it, or any part of my body, really.

I blinked and blinked some more until I could semi-focus, and saw a man dressed in black hurrying into the room.

I swallowed down the bile when the man hooked his arm around Cobie's limp form, followed shortly by Mary's.

And I realized rather quickly that what was happening shouldn't be happening. The man dressed in black, Drake Garwood, shouldn't be here.

I also should be moving, yet I couldn't get my limbs to cooperate.

I clenched my hand and felt my fingers close around something— my phone.

Yet, still, I couldn't get my fingers to execute my mind's commands.

I couldn't get anything to work. Not my hands, not my legs, and definitely not my brain.

Which had to be why I watched him walk out the door without so much as a single protest from me.

And I realized then that I'd spread myself too thin.

I thought I could help. I thought I could be there to protect them— like I should've protected my sister all those years ago—but I didn't.

I started to crawl, ordering myself harshly under my breath to go.

Go, go, go.

And somehow, I went.

It was sometime later when my brain started to slowly come back online.

A stun grenade.

He'd thrown a stun grenade—Drake had.

He'd thrown it through the window, and when it went off, I'd reacted exactly like he had expected I would—for the most part.

I was fairly sure he hadn't expected me to be coherent enough to actually follow.

Which had to be why he didn't once look in his rearview mirror.

Blood was running freely from the wound on my scalp. It was running in my eyes, down my cheeks, around my nose to disappear into my chin. Only, it came right back out to run down my neck.

I was fairly sure I had a broken collarbone, as well as a concussion.

But I'd managed to drive behind Cobie and Mary's captor—Drake.

I'd also been able to stay hidden.

I'd called for help, and I'd forced my body to stay where it was.

I wasn't fooling anyone—not even myself.

The moment I got out of this car, I knew that I'd collapse to my knees.

I knew, without a shadow of a doubt, that my legs would give out, and I'd crumple to the ground like a useless heap of trash.

Did that stop me from getting out of the car, though?

Hell no.

It sure the fuck didn't.

It also didn't stop me from running—or maybe limping, I wasn't quite sure—toward the guardrail where Drake had just pushed Cobie's car over the bridge.

It hit the water below with a huge splash, and vaguely I watched as Cobie came to consciousness as the jolt of the car hitting the water jarred her awake.

I'd just reached the bridge when I heard, rather than saw, a large truck heading toward us.

Just when I made the decision to jump, I saw a truck pass—a car on a chain directly behind it—headed straight for Drake who was now laughing.

He'd seen me. He'd seen the state he'd left me in. And he knew, as well as I did, that I was about to make the last decision I'd ever have to make.

I had enough in me to get them out. I knew it.

I'd make it happen.

I would.

And then I hit the water feet first.

The cool water, a huge contrast from the humid air, surrounded me. Revived me.

I swam toward the car, which was sinking nose first.

I didn't go to Cobie's seat. I went to the back seat and started to yank on the door.

"The locks! Unlock it!"

Cobie's head turned, and she hit the locks.

The moment the door was unlocked, I yanked at the handle, pulling with everything I had to get the door open.

It didn't so much as budge.

I braced both feet on either side of the door and pulled hard, but it didn't help.

The door wasn't going to open, and it was sinking too fast for me to do a damn thing about it.

"Move," Dante growled.

I did and felt myself weaken even further.

Then, before I could do anything more, I sank into oblivion.

CHAPTER 8

Apparently when the salesperson asked if I needed help finding anything, the correct answer was not 'my soulmate and cheap liquor.'
Who knew?

Janie

"Hello?" I answered, looking at my phone at the same time I took a bite of my pickle.

I liked pickles. Sue me.

"Janie," Kayla whispered. "I think you need to get down to the command center…something's happened."

I got up, taking my pickle with me, and headed for the front door, not bothering to change.

"What's going on?" I asked as I reached for the doorknob.

"There's something going on with Rafe."

And that was the last coherent thought I had for the next eight hours.

***

I rubbed my fingers along the space between my eyebrows and tried not to throw up.

"Daddy," I pleaded. "His phone is about six miles downstream. I swear to God, he's there."

My father looked at me with pity-filled eyes.

"They've already swept that area, Janie. He's not there."

"He has to be there," I replied stubbornly. "His phone would be in the water. It's not in the water. It's on the bank!"

"They've already done all the searching they're going to do tonight," he whispered so that only I could hear. "Baby, you need to calm down."

No one, in the history of the world, has ever calmed down by being told to calm down.

Just sayin'.

"Fine," I said through gritted teeth. "I'll do it myself."

I turned to leave, and my father caught my arm before I could so much as take a step away from him.

Then he went and did what fathers do and pulled me to the stairwell moments later, which worked for me because that's where I wanted to go.

I didn't, however, want to stop just outside the door.

"What the fuck?" he asked. "What's your damn deal?"

"What's my deal?" I semi-shrieked. "Rafe is missing, and none of you are doing a damn thing about it!"

"None of us...Janie, what the hell do you think you're going to accomplish by going at night?" he said, his voice getting softer.

I hated it when his voice got softer. It made me realize that he actually cared. That maybe, just maybe, he was right.

I swallowed tears.

"I have to look for him. I have to find him," I replied, my voice breaking. "I have—"

A commotion had my dad looking over his shoulder, and then he moved to pull the door of the stairwell open.

"Get a nurse!" a man bellowed. "*Rafe!* Rafe, look at me buddy."

I started running before I'd consciously told my feet to start moving.

Then, I was skidding on my knees beside Rafe who was laying on the floor, looking deathly pale.

He was wet. His head was still bleeding, and when I pressed my hand to his face, I could feel his fever raging.

"Rafe," I breathed, leaning forward.

His eyes opened a fraction of an inch, and I swallowed at the dark eyes that met my own.

"Rafe," I repeated.

He blinked.

Then he smiled.

After that, his entire form went limp.

***

Nine and a half hours later

Rafe was better.

He wasn't awake, but he was stable.

His fever was down, the swelling on the side of his face was decreasing, and his color was starting to return to normal.

I swallowed the bile that rose in my throat, again, as the doctor shook his head.

"Is he okay?" I asked the doctor.

"His pupils are reacting, which means that he's responding. He's likely not awake yet due to the trauma that he received from the concussion grenade," the doctor explained. "Sometimes all the body needs is time to recover. Maybe he just needs the sleep."

I kept my mouth shut, and only nodded my head. Afraid if I spoke that the wounded cry that I'd been keeping bottled the entire time I'd been here would fall from my lips.

"If he wakes, come find us." Then he was gone just as fast as he'd arrived.

I looked from the door where the doctor had just disappeared to the man lying so still in the bed.

He looked wrong.

I'd never seen him so still.

It was disconcerting.

Normally Rafe was so full of life—his aura almost chokingly powerful.

Now…now he just felt so…gone.

I closed my eyes and dropped my head into my hands, blowing out a breath.

"Hurry up and wake up," I breathed. "You're scaring me."

Just as I'd finished that sentence, the door to the hospital room opened, and a woman blew in.

She was tall, willowy, and beautiful. She had long brown hair, bright blue eyes, and an obvious way about her that practically screamed 'I've got money!'

I, on the other hand, was on the shorter side of average. I had long blonde hair that rarely ever found its way out of a ponytail, hazel eyes that kind of looked like pond water, and a face that wasn't much to look at.

This woman was everything I wasn't.

Everything that I thought Rafe would go for.

And I'd seen her before.

This was pecan pie chick.

"Oh, Rafe!" she breathed as she caught sight of the man in the bed. "You poor thing! Daddy told me that you were in here, and I didn't believe him. I just had to see for myself. Oh, gosh. Are you even awake?"

"He's in a coma," I murmured, bringing her attention to me for the first time.

She blinked and stared. "Who are you?" she sneered.

I would've laughed at her obvious outrage at seeing me in Rafe's room—past hours—but I couldn't even find the strength to pick up my head from my hands.

"I'm Janie," I answered.

"The daughter of a friend," she said. "I remember you. The hair."

She gestured to her head, miming hair in a bun, and I grimaced. "Yes."

I guess you could consider me a daughter of a friend...technically.

Though, I wouldn't go as far as to call them 'friends.'

Acquaintances, maybe. Friends, no.

"Right," she said, then moved to the bed. "What are you doing here?"

"What am I doing here?" I asked, sounding as offended as I felt. "What are you doing here?"

I narrowed my eyes. "I'm here because Rafe is hurt."

"So am I," she challenged.

I clenched my teeth.

"I'm a *really* good friend," I said. "Rafe's never even mentioned you."

The woman in front of me smiled. "Funny," she drawled. "But he's never once mentioned you, either. And we've spent quite a bit of time together over the last six weeks."

Then she did something that had the breath leaving my lungs.

She held out her hand. "I'm officially the soon to be Mrs. Rafe."

My jaw would've hit the floor if it wasn't attached.

"You're lying," I whispered, feeling suddenly sick to my stomach.

"I have absolutely no reason to lie," she crossed her arms. "I can tell you exactly where he's been for the last six weeks…can you?"

No. No, I fucking couldn't.

"What the fuck?"

I looked down at a now awake Rafe, seeing his eyes were just barely slitted, but very much aware.

"Oh, honey."

I winced and backed away when Mrs. Soon-to-be Rafe slammed her purse the size of a small horse into my chest.

Oh, honey, I mimicked, crossing my arms and glaring at the stupid woman's perfectly coifed hair.

Rafe saw me, and he frowned.

"Who are y'all, and why are y'all here?"

Something cold slithered down my spine.

"Who are we?" I said, confusion lacing my voice. "Rafe, do you not know who I am?"

His jerked his head away from the girl that was petting his beard like one would a dog and growled at her. "Stop touching me."

The woman stopped, but she didn't pull away altogether. Instead, she turned so that she could stare at me.

"You're no longer needed. I'm here."

I opened my mouth to tell her that under no uncertain terms was I leaving when the door was pushed open.

"Oh, you're awake!"

I turned to find myself staring at a nurse, who was staring at me and Hooters girl with a frown.

"I'm sorry, but there is only one visitor allowed back here at a time. This floor's rules. I'm sorry."

"As his fiancée, I'm staying."

I opened my mouth to argue that she could kiss my fat ass when the nurse turned to me. "And who are you to him?"

"He can't remember who we are," I blurted. "Is that normal?"

The nurse turned to Rafe.

"Do you know who these ladies are?" she questioned.

Rafe shook his head, barely hiding the wince in time.

I saw it, though.

Then again, there wasn't a single thing about Rafe that I didn't notice or know…at least I thought there wasn't, anyway.

"No," Rafe murmured, sounding like he was getting angry. "Should I?"

And that was when I realized that things were bad. Really, really bad.

"Who do you want to stay?" the nurse asked. "There can only be one."

Rafe's eyes bounced from me to the woman at his side, then

moved back.

They stayed locked on me, and for a second, I saw recognition there.

Then, it was gone.

"Neither."

"Okay then," the nurse said. "Both of you out."

I felt like I'd been punched in the stomach.

But nonetheless, I walked out, not stopping until I was two doors down from his room.

"Don't think that just because you knew him before me that you can worm your way in there," the snotty female voice let me know that I hadn't left by myself. The she-devil had left, too.

I turned and glared. "I'm sorry. Did I miss the fact that I was talking to you?"

"He's mine."

I bared my teeth.

"If he's yours, he'll be yours." I paused. "But, just being honest, the moment that he regains his memory, you're not going to get rid of me so easily."

She laughed. "We'll see about that, now won't we?

It wasn't until she left that I lost my battle with the tears.

Moments later, my father rounded the corner of the hallway and looked at me, noting the tears almost immediately.

"Ready?"

I felt betrayed. I felt stupid. And honestly, I felt like I was the world's dumbest person.

While I was waiting for him to uncomplicate his life, he was out getting engaged.

God, I was so fucking *stupid!*

"Janie…" my father said. "You ready to go? There's nothing you can do here to help."

I would've laughed at that had I not just thought the same thing.

"Yeah, Dad," I murmured softly. "I'll come back tomorrow. Maybe then I can get some answers."

Only, the next day didn't go any better.

Or the day after that.

Or the day after that.

Then, the icing on the cake was when the doctor came out and told us—with Rafe's blessing of course, since he didn't want to see us, but he knew that we'd want to know his prognosis—the other news. News that changed my entire life.

He had an inoperable brain aneurysm, and under no circumstances was he to be upset in *any* way.

If he *did* get upset, stressed, or excited, that could mean the end of his life.

Which only left me even more depressed. If I couldn't remind him who I was—which might very well upset him and stress him out— then what else could I do? What choice did I have?

There was only one.

Leave him alone with the hope that he'd figure it out on his own.

Lani Lynn Vale

CHAPTER 9

I solemnly swear I'm going to rock your world until we're old and dead.
-Rafe to Janie

Rafe

I knew a few things.

One, I knew why I was where I was.

Two, I knew that Angelina Jolie, I mean my fake kind of real fiancée, Elspeth, was playing me just as much as I was playing her.

Three, I knew there was something there with Janie, but I couldn't quite figure out what it was.

Which happened to be why I was where I was.

I needed to talk to my sister.

I knew, without a shadow of a doubt, that I would've told her what was going on.

Ever since she'd let me back into her life, I hadn't held a single thing back.

Not one single thing.

At least, I thought I hadn't.

"I'm sure, Rafe," my sister, Raven, promised, looking guilty as hell about something. Yet, I knew from experience that she wouldn't tell me what that something was. If she wanted to share, she would. Obviously, she didn't want to share, otherwise the words would've been out of her mouth the moment I'd walked in the door. "I don't know anything about any girls. Nothing."

I growled under my breath and rubbed my hand over my heart.

"You're going to get it back," Raven promised. "And when you do, if it was meant to be, whoever the girl is will still be waiting for you."

My sister's words felt like sandpaper against my soul. She may be saying all the right things, but I still couldn't quite believe them.

"I don't know anything that has happened in the last six months," I said, staring pointedly at my sister's belly.

Raven started to grin. "Four months ago, brother. And I hadn't actually told you about this one. I was waiting for you to come see me…and you never did."

I grunted and looked out at the parking lot.

We met for lunch—halfway between her and me—and she'd chosen the spot.

I hated Mexican food—yes, I know. I can hear your shouts of denial and dismay from here—but it was what it was.

And it wasn't even the taste that I didn't like.

It was the smell.

My father had once forced me to drink an entire bottle of hot sauce—one of those small jars that you get at the grocery store—because I'd wasted the food he'd bought.

And me, being young and impressionable at the time, had done it despite my monumental dislike of the sauce.

After drinking it, I'd immediately thrown up.

All over the floor and half the couch.

My father had back handed me so hard and fast that I'd landed on my back in the middle of my vomit and learned a very important lesson.

It would never do to show weakness.

Hence the reason I did what I did hours later when Elspeth showed at my door.

I took the pecan pie inside, allowed Elspeth to follow me, and choked down two pieces of the vile crap with her watching.

Once she'd gone, I'd immediately tossed the rest of the pie. Then brushed my teeth to get rid of the taste.

All the while I wondered if Janie knew I didn't like pecans.

She probably did.

Yet, I couldn't quite figure out why I cared.

Yet, every single time I found my mind wandering, I found it centered on her.

On what she was thinking. Or feeling. Or even doing.

Anything about her would suffice.

Which was why I'd also hacked into her computer and started

watching her through her webcam installed on her laptop.

A laptop that she spent an exceptionally insane amount of time on.

There wasn't a single instance that I'd logged in that I didn't see her on it. Didn't watch her every fucking move.

It was seriously starting to get to the point where I felt sick—at myself.

I was invading her privacy.

I was watching her work.

I was reading things that I shouldn't be reading.

Yet I couldn't stop.

I couldn't stop because there was this compulsion inside of me that was urging me to do it.

Like right this second, I was watching her bite her lip as she watched a Hallmark movie—which I could hear running in the background. She was switching between playing on Facebook and Instagram, intermittently glancing up at the TV when something caught her attention.

I couldn't figure out if she was crying because of what she was watching on the TV or if there was something else that she was thinking about.

Whatever it was, I felt sick to my stomach.

I didn't like to see her cry, and I most certainly didn't want her doing it in the dark of her living room while she sat there looking so sad and lonely.

I wanted to ride over there and wrap her in my arms—even though

I didn't understand why.

Which made me mad.

Every single thing there was to know about this woman—Janie—was gone. None of it was there.

Apparently, according to Trace, I'd known Janie for a really long time.

Really long meaning years and years.

But that was all Trace had given me.

He'd clammed up the moment I'd tried to dig for more.

In fact, everyone had.

I'd even gone as far as to ask James, Janie's father, and I was left in the dark.

It was really starting to irritate me.

Speaking of irritants, my phone rang, and I lifted it up off the couch at my side and placed it to my ear.

"Yeah?" I muttered, recognizing Trace's ringtone.

"You got a bug in the church?"

I rolled my eyes. "You know I do."

After my accident, I'd been busting my ass to get myself up to speed with the investigation I'd started—one that was very near and dear to my heart.

Layton Trammel, the man who had singlehandedly left me a near eunuch. My balls were very near and dear to me…literally and figuratively.

And Layton had been such a dick about it.

When I'd tried to file malpractice after I'd recovered enough, I'd gotten a strong lecture from my CO that I needed to 'forget it and move on.'

When I'd pursued, I'd been given another lecture, this one consisting of me being told that if I didn't 'cease and desist,' I would regret it.

I almost did because I'd tried to pursue it, nearly receiving a dishonorable discharge for my efforts.

And so, the feud had been born.

"Yeah, well, Layton just made a stop over there. He's talking with a deacon for their church, and he's got a lot of good stuff to say about you. He thinks you're going to be the 'perfect goat.'

"Goat," I repeated, making sure I'd heard him correctly.

"Goat," he repeated, "As in 'scapegoat.'"

I gritted my teeth. "Scapegoat for what?"

"I don't know. But they've been talking about a few things for about seven minutes now. They want to meet up later on to confirm details. That *later on* being some time tonight after dinner with you."

"I wasn't aware I was having dinner with him…"

"Well, I'd wait and not make any plans. I'd also play nice and say you can come despite your immediate reaction of 'go fuck yourself.' Okay?" Trace added gruffly.

I snorted.

The man knew me so well.

"Yeah," I grumbled, my eyes going to the laptop again. She'd gotten up and moved out of the screen. "Did you find out anything else about the girl and our engagement?"

"You weren't engaged the last time we spoke before your accident," Trace answered hesitantly. "But you also said you'd found out something, so maybe in order to get that information, you got engaged to the chick. I don't know, man. I'll keep an ear to the ground, though. We'll get you out of this."

I heard him say something else under his breath, and I strained to hear what he said, but I could barely make it out.

He'd been doing that a lot. Saying things softly, as if he wanted to tell me something but couldn't quite work up the nerve.

Him, and everyone else.

I could've sworn it had something to do with 'stubborn girls,' though.

"All right," I finally sighed. "But Trace, if there's something you need to tell me, you should tell me now. I know I'm missing something here."

"Did you ask your sister?"

"Yeah," I grumbled. "She had no clue I'd even had a girl in my life. Which then pissed her off all over again because I wasn't coming home enough."

Trace started to chuckle, then sobered. "Don't beat yourself up. You've bridged that gap with her, but it's her that has to take that last step. You can't do it all."

No, I couldn't.

But the guilt was never-ending.

My sister had been in a bad situation…then again, so had I.

It was either leave her behind, where I had the promise that she would be happy and healthy or take her with me and run.

And running was no place for a child.

She grew up happy—ish. She grew up healthy.

And she'd found the love of her life…which was more than I could say for me.

The doors to my room pushed open and my doctor appeared, smiling at me as he came.

His eyes took in the laptop in my lap, as well as the phone to my ear, and he frowned.

"All right, man," I said with a sigh. "I'm about to get sprung. You decide to tell me what I'm missing, I'd love it."

Trace hung up laughing.

I hung up pissed off.

Which didn't bode well for the doctor when he told me he wanted me to stay another night.

"No," I refused. "I'm not running a fever, I have a very mild concussion, and I have shit to do that doesn't include me staying here."

"It's okay, Ross." Another man pushed through my open hospital door. "I'm taking him home with me tonight."

Layton Trammel.

I'd know that pretty face anywhere.

I wonder if he *knew* that I wasn't going to be sprung today without supervision.

Did he have anything to do with this or was it all his daughter's doing?

The questions that sprang to mind nearly made my head spin.

Did he recognize me? Did he know that his girl and I were 'engaged?'

Dr. Ross sighed. "As long as he's under supervision, I don't mind him going home."

I would've gone home whether he wanted me to or not…

"He'll be with me, and my girl. My girl is exceptionally worried about him," Layton drawled, his eyes coming to me.

I felt like an oily hand had just run down my arm, causing the hair on my arm to be rubbed the wrong way.

Yay.

I got to spend time with my worst enemy. *The* enemy. And the icing on the cake was that he has no fucking clue that I was someone he knew.

As if he'd fucked over so many people that I wasn't even on his radar any longer.

It was goddamn annoying, was what it was.

Common decency would've been him at least remembering nearly taking a man's ability to reproduce.

To give the man credit, though, I'd changed a lot from that little grunt that I'd been as a new recruit. The one he'd known.

This Rafe, the new Rafe? Nobody knew this Rafe.

And I'd be keeping it that way.

She knows you.

That stray thought felt like a lead anvil hitting me straight in the chest.

Nobody would ever know me like that—which was why I slammed the laptop shut and didn't bother opening it back up again.

Not for a very long time.

Which was a huge fucking mistake.

CHAPTER 10

I have the patience of a saint. Saint Cunt McFuckoff.
-Coffee Cup

Rafe

Three weeks later

I went home to what should have been my empty house and instead found the she-devil standing at my door.

She had a baking dish in her hands, and she was smiling at me with a smile so white and bright that it was blinding.

I really, really disliked her.

But, after talking to Trace, I realized that I'd been working a job.

She was part of that job.

Lucky for me I'd been sharing my findings with Trace, otherwise, I'd be just as lost here with him as I was with the Janie girl.

The Janie girl that nobody seemed to want to tell me about.

It'd been a long three weeks, and still, to this day, I'd gotten nothing out of my friend.

Why, I couldn't quite figure, but even Trace—my old good

friend—wouldn't say a word.

And when I asked, he'd give me the same spiel he'd given me the first time. "You'll know when you're meant to know, and not a moment before."

The doctors had told me not to push my memory.

I'd remember when I remembered and pushing could actually set my recovery back even further.

Which I thought was a crock of shit, but again, I wasn't the expert. Or, at least, that was what Trace kept telling me.

"Whatcha got there?" I called as I put the kickstand up on my bike.

Yes, I'd ridden the bike home in the middle of a rainstorm.

Seemed only fair

Angelina She-Devil Jolie, also known as Elspeth Trammel, smiled sweetly at me. "Pecan pie."

Gross.

I grimaced and tried to give her a smile, but I couldn't hack it.

"I'm sorry, Elspeth, but I'm not feeling all that well…" and I wasn't. "I'm gonna have to take a shower and maybe go to bed. Can we do dinner tomorrow to make up for it?"

Elspeth frowned and scooted closer, bringing the smell of her disgusting pie with her.

The feeling of her hand on my hand felt like poison on my skin.

I'd watched a movie the night before on my phone during a stakeout of the Trammel residence, and a certain scene came to mind. The main two characters that were running for their lives through the woods and were being complete dumbasses about it.

They should've stayed where they were because they had protection at their backs, weapons at their fronts, light so they could see and strength in their numbers. But they decided to split up, two and two. Then they all ran into the fucking woods where it was dark, split up, and never once thought about looking up with their flashlights.

So, there they were, running with their stupid flashlights that barely illuminated three feet in front of them, and not goddamn once did they think to look up until they felt the alien's saliva drip on their skin.

The alien's saliva burned like acid…which was what Elspeth's touch was reminding me of.

I pulled my arm back. "You should probably not get too close. Germs."

She smiled at my suggestion.

"If I get sick, then you can just take care of me," she suggested.

Yeah, fucking right.

I didn't take care of anybody.

Except for maybe Janie.

She'd look *a-fucking-dorable* sick.

I'd totally sit next to her and willingly be in her germ zone.

Why? I couldn't tell you.

Which immediately pissed me off.

"Take care of yourself, Luis."

Luis.

I gave her a fake smile and wrapped her in my arms, even though I felt like vomiting into her hair when her lips pressed against my neck.

To keep my mind off of the state of my stomach, I allowed my eyes to roam around the street, my eyes spotting a familiar car.

"I'll see you tomorrow, sweetheart," she whispered, pulling away.

Then she left with a small wave, leaving the stupid pie behind.

I didn't so much as wait for her to get to her car before I headed inside and went straight to the bathroom for the shower that I'd been speaking of.

Once I had my clothes off, I got in the shower, my thoughts drifting to the car.

It was a familiar car, but I couldn't say how I knew it.

Something about that car, though, brought up the stirring of memories that was making my heart pound.

And that pounding only showed up when I thought about *her*.

Janie.

***

Janie

The entire ride over I'd berated myself for showing up unannounced, but I had to talk to him. I had to know. I had to see.

What I saw made me realize that what I had with Rafe was gone.

He may not remember me, but he sure looked like he remembered her.

They looked happy.

I felt like my heart had just been ripped from my chest. As if someone had reached in, gripped it in their large fist, and squeezed as they ripped.

I didn't look back as I started my car.

I didn't think about him while I drove.

And I definitely didn't think about his favorite coffee when I walked into my favorite little hole in the wall coffee shop that reminded me of him.

No. Not one single bit.

Also, that was a lie.

Everything was a lie.

I wasn't sure that anything would ever be the truth again.

CHAPTER 11

Home: where the ho & me come together.
-Welcome Mat

Janie

One month later

It started out as an accident, at least on my part.

At first, I'd said yes to the coffee because he'd looked lost.

The day that I'd shown up for my coffee after seeing Rafe with that woman, I'd been lost. I must've looked lost, too, because a kindred soul had found me standing there. He'd asked to have a seat, and I'd shrugged.

I hadn't really wanted to be alone, and this guy seemed harmless.

Wrong.

The second coffee date, I couldn't get out of there fast enough either.

But, as the coffee dates wore on, I realized that they weren't *too* bad. If he was lonely, who was I not to share a coffee with him? I was literally at the coffee shop anyway.

It was on the fifteenth such coffee date that he'd brought his mother. He'd brought his mother to introduce her to his girlfriend. Apparently, that would be me.

What the fuck?

Kayla had nearly cried as I'd recounted what had happened that day.

"You're joking, right?" she'd wheezed. "Oh my God. You're going to be stuck with the asshole forever if you don't fix this right now."

I had no idea how right she was.

See, in my quest to get over Rafe, I'd created a monster. A monster that talked, breathed, and spoke to me.

Tegan Aggrad, a twenty-eight-year-old police officer who worked with my father, wasn't what I was looking for.

Yet, in my grief over what I'd seen with Rafe, I let it go too far.

"You want to meet my dad," I said, surprised.

"Yes," he said.

"You've already met him," I told Tegan.

Yes, as my boyfriend, they hadn't met.

But, at work, they had.

They knew of each other. They just hadn't met each other outside of work in the form of us being boyfriend and girlfriend.

"Okay," I hesitated. "Tomorrow?"

He shook his head. "Now."

"Now," I repeated, sounding like a parrot. "Ummm," I hesitated. "I'm not sure if my dad's home."

He gave me a look that clearly said that I was purposefully stalling…which I was.

I didn't want Tegan to come to my house. I most certainly didn't want to introduce him to my family.

Yet, I couldn't say no.

He gave me those puppy dog eyes, and I felt terrible.

"Fine," I shrugged. "Let's go. You can follow me home."

Tegan opened his mouth to argue, but I cut him off.

I knew exactly what he was going to say, "Let me take you home."

My reply was always the same. "You're not taking me home because I'm not leaving my car here."

Yet, when I told him that, he'd then say, "Well you should've let me pick you up."

Which I would then reply with, "I don't want to be stuck there in case someone needs me."

It always happened like that. Always.

So, I chose to circumvent it by getting into my car and slamming the door shut, effectively cutting him off before he could say anything more that had the possibility to annoy me.

He sighed and turned to leave, and I felt the nervous tick start.

I didn't want him to come to meet my dad.

I didn't want him to see where I lived, and I most certainly didn't want to do anything that had to do with him getting any closer to me.

My house was my space. My sanctuary, and I didn't want him in it.

Yet, as I pulled out of the driveway of the coffee shop, I didn't speed in front of him so he couldn't follow me home—though he probably knew where I lived as did the rest of the people in Kilgore.

Everything was okay, at least I felt like I was handling it okay until I pulled up to the gate that led inside and saw the familiar bike parked next to it.

I swallowed thickly as I pressed the opener and the gate started to slide open.

The man on the bike turned his head and looked at me, causing my breath to hitch.

I hadn't seen him in a month, yet it felt like only seconds had passed.

He was still just as hot as he was the last time I saw him, though he had a scar on his forehead that came down out of his hairline thanks to being thrown across the room all those weeks ago.

"Janie," he stared.

My heart soared as I thought he might've remembered, but when nothing more was forthcoming, I realized that he hadn't remembered me. In fact, I was fairly certain he was just being nice as he said hello to someone.

"Hi," I smiled…or tried to anyway. "Can't get in?"

He shook his head. "Rang the bell. Have some news. Been sitting here for about fifteen minutes now."

I fucking hated my family sometimes.

They thought it was funny, leaving him outside like this.

Yet it wasn't funny.

It pissed me off.

Greatly.

"Who is this?" Tegan's voice came from behind me, causing me to jump in my seat.

I leaned a little farther out of my car to see Tegan standing beside his open door, his arms crossed tightly over his chest.

I could practically read the anger rolling off of him as he stared at Rafe, who hadn't been startled by Tegan's appearance, and who also was still semi slouched on his bike looking bored.

"This is Rafe," I said. "Head on in. The door will close in about thirty seconds."

Rafe didn't bother to waste time. He dropped his foot, leaned the bike up straight, and then kicked the kickstand back before starting it up.

The familiar roar of the bike had me smiling as I watched him ride inside, and when I followed shortly after him, I completely missed the anger that flashed in Tegan's eyes.

I also missed the way his hands fisted, mostly because I was staring at the back of Rafe's head.

He looked good.

Very good.

And my heart fucking hurt just having him in the same vicinity as me.

I wanted him more than I wanted my next breath.

*****

Rafe

I clocked him out of the corner of my eye as he'd pulled in, but my entire being had been solely focused on the woman. Janie.

I had forced myself not to look at her, check up on her, or see her for the last month purely because I knew that I didn't need to be doing what I was doing.

I still hadn't remembered anything about our time together—and I knew for certain we'd spent some time together.

One didn't feel this strongly about a person if there'd only been an introduction.

Yet, nobody said a word to me about Janie. In fact, she was never brought up. Not ever.

Not when I was in the room with her father and the rest of the men of Free. Not when I spoke with Trace, and most certainly not now when she was standing there looking at me.

I got off my bike and waited for Janie to get out of her car—a car that looked familiar, yet I couldn't figure out why.

"Come on," she gestured to me, heading for the door to the offices.

I'd been here before, of course, but nothing felt familiar as I walked with them.

"How's Elspeth?" Janie asked, sounding like she'd rather be asking anything other than that.

"Fine," I murmured, annoyed to hear about my fake fiancé. "She's working."

Janie's face fell.

"Why do I feel like I know you?" I whispered.

Her eyes widened. "Because you…"

"Janie," Tegan, the twat whistle, called. "I'd like to meet your dad before I have to go to work."

I gritted my teeth as her eyes widened. "Do you need Uncle Sam? Or do you need them all?"

I clearly read the change in subject. "One of them is fine for now," I offered.

Janie grinned. "My dad is on his way."

"That's fine," I murmured.

"Your dad will be here soon?" Tegan asked, even though Janie had just stated that fact.

"He's coming," Janie snapped. "He said he'd be here in about five minutes. He was walking my dogs for me."

Dogs.

Speaking of dogs, I could hear the barking coming from the opposite direction.

I turned and saw James topping a hill in the distance, two German Shepherds at his sides.

"You didn't tell me you had dogs," the douche said, sounding worried.

"I didn't?" Janie asked. "Huh, must've slipped my mind."

The dogs started running, and when they were close enough, started to lick Janie all over.

They stayed well away from Tegan, but the surprise wasn't that they did that, but when they instead came to me.

They went back and forth between Janie and me, licking and yipping, and I wasn't the only one to notice.

James, Janie's father, and Tegan—her pitiful excuse for a boyfriend—had, too.

My hand went down to the dog who was incredibly familiar with me, and I smoothed my hand down her face.

"Glock," I heard Janie say. "That one that Rafe is petting is Kimber."

Tegan crossed his arms over his chest when the dog closest to Janie got too close.

"You don't like dogs?" I found myself asking.

"No," Tegan denied. "I don't like slobber."

I looked down at the dogs that were leaking like sieves after their walk, and grinned.

I had slobber on my hands and my pants, as did Janie.

"Huh," I said, grinning.

Janie smiled at me. "They're definitely droolers. Just wait until I give them a rawhide. They'll go all crazy and slobber on you."

"Negative," Tegan shook his head. Moments later his eyes lifted to the man that had stopped at my side.

James didn't seem to reciprocate. "Yeah, hi, Tegan."

"Janie, honey, why don't you go put your dogs up? They're probably thirsty. We've been outside a lot today," James murmured, keeping his eyes on Tegan.

I could practically feel the tension in him.

It would've been amusing had he not been there to see *her*.

Janie gave her father a thumb up, and moments later called to her dogs as she started walking away.

My eyes automatically went to Janie's ass, but quickly moved away when I saw James turn his eyes toward me.

"You mind waiting inside?"

I shrugged and headed that way but stopped right inside the door when I heard Tegan say, "Nice to see you again."

It wasn't Tegan's remark, but James' reply that had me smirking. "I can't say the same."

My lips quirked.

"I came over today to introduce myself and to let you know that I'm in love with your daughter."

Something inside of me went still as his words penetrated my brain.

I'm in love with your daughter.

Six words. Twenty-four letters.

One shot to the heart.

"Is that so," James drawled.

Please, say it isn't so.

"Yes, sir," Tegan replied. "I'm glad that we're getting to meet. I wanted you to know how I felt about your daughter and to ask you a question."

Fuck.

I had a feeling that it was coming.

"I have a feeling you'll be happy," Tegan replied, sounding entirely too smug for my liking.

"I can't say that the feeling is a good one," I heard James counter.

I leaned my back against the wall and let my head fall to the cool wood behind me, closing my eyes as I waited for the inevitable.

"I want to ask your permission to marry…"

"No."

I would've hooted in laughter at James' quick denial, but I couldn't let on that I was listening.

"James…"

"I said no. You're not going to get my permission. I assume you're going to ask her anyway, but let me be clear, I don't like you. You haven't known her for but a month, and to be honest, I'm not even sure she likes you," James continued as if Tegan wasn't standing right in front of him. "You fucked me over during that investigation, and I can tell you now that I will never think you're good enough for her. You're a piece of slime, and my heart will literally break if she says yes to you. But for her? If you're who she chooses? I'll learn to live with it. I just want you to know I won't ever like you."

Tegan said nothing.

Then I heard Janie's, "Dad?" And I knew why nothing was said in reply.

Tegan didn't seem the type to let something like that go.

The little asshole.

God, I felt like something was breaking inside of me.

"Yeah, baby?" James called.

I opened the door so I could see the scene in front of me.

Janie's eyes immediately came to me, completely forgoing the other two men that were closer to her.

And this also didn't go by unnoticed by Tegan the slime bag, either.

He narrowed his eyes at me as if he was mortally offended not to have Janie's complete undivided attention, which then caused me to grin.

Tegan narrowed his eyes even farther.

"Janie?"

Janie had to peel her eyes from me, and the moment her eyes were slid away, I felt like half of my soul was gone along with her gaze.

"You ready?" James asked, looking in my direction.

I nodded, then reluctantly turned and walked back into the room.

Instinctively I knew where to go, even though a lot of this was still unfamiliar to me—at least the new me.

"You okay?"

I looked up to find James staring at me.

"This not knowing where to go, but knowing where to go thing, is like a fucking tick in my brain. Like I know, but I just can't get it to fully form. It's driving me insane," I explained.

James nodded. "Sure, it sucks. Why are you here?"

I crossed my arms over my chest. "I need some monitoring done on a few individuals. One in particular. I've been sitting on him for months now, and I'm not getting anything. I've gotten to know the daughter trying to get a closer look, but there's nothing there. Even though I know for a fact that this guy is dealing with things that could be huge."

"What kind of huge?" James asked.

"The kind of huge that will blow a hole in a corruption case the size that the US Military has never seen," I answered.

James blinked. "What is it that you do again?"

I grinned. "I do what I want."

James' eyes narrowed. "Like date a girl, ask her to marry you, and fuck her over while you try to send her father to prison?"

There was some underlying hostility there, and I knew that he knew something. Something that I still didn't know.

"You have something you want to say to me?" I asked carefully.

James shrugged. "I was told that you would figure it out on your own time. I just hope when you figure it out it's not too late."

That cryptic statement helped zero.

Goddamn them.

"James…"

"Janie's really good with computers."

I knew that, because I was, too.

She'd been trying to figure out something that had changed on her computer for a while now, and I knew that eventually she'd figure it out.

My only hope was that she wouldn't be completely pissed when she found out.

To be honest, I really didn't need their help.

I just needed their backup in the instance that my case went to shit.

Normally I wouldn't need help at all, but then again, I'd never had to deal with a man the likes of Layton Trammel before.

He was suspicious, tenacious and careful. So careful, in fact, that I had a feeling that any dealings he had at all with whomever he was selling and buying from was done through a third party. Some man, or men, helped him. Someone big who knew what the fuck they were doing.

And I wanted the backup and the extra set of eyes.

The men of Free weren't the only ones I asked, either.

I'd also had my brother-in-law, Wolf, keeping an eye out, too.

I was officially asking for help.

And that was unheard of for me.

Trace and I had been it for a really long time now, so it was hard to branch out and extend that hand.

But I'd do it because this was the last job I'd be doing before I officially closed that chapter of my life. The chapter that had shaped me into the man I was today.

"You okay?"

James had apparently been talking to me.

"Yeah," I said. "Just fucking tired."

And I was. All the goddamn time.

"Did you hear what I said about Janie?"

I nodded at his question. "I did, but I won't be asking her for help."

"Why?" he pushed.

I frowned. "Because this job is big. The man I'm investigating, he's a heavy hitter. I don't doubt that Janie's good, but this man isn't anyone to fuck with. He's the man that nearly cost me my life ten years ago, and he's hurt so many more."

"I'm not a child."

I looked up to find Janie in the room.

Tegan was nowhere to be seen, but that wasn't to say that he was gone.

Moments later, he filled the door frame and looked around like he'd never been inside here before.

"Janie, there are rules," James said, eyeing Tegan behind her.

"Shit, sorry," she said, looking sheepish.

Moments later she herded the fool out the door, even though it was more than obvious that he didn't want to go.

"There are rules?" I questioned James when she'd left.

"Yeah, the kind of rules that say no dumbasses allowed in places they shouldn't be in," James grunted.

I smirked. "Don't like him?"

James didn't bother to act like he'd misunderstood my question. "Can't fucking stand him. He was the investigator for a shooting that I was involved in, and let's just say things could have gone better."

Interesting.

I'd be looking into that.

"Anyway, what I was saying was that I don't want her involved. This needs to be done by someone that knows what they're doing. She's got skills, but she doesn't have those years of experience that Jack has."

"I can do anything that Jack does, if not better."

Janie again.

I sighed.

I was really getting soft in my old age.

I hadn't even heard the door open.

James' lips quirked.

"Maybe y'all should go outside and have a talk. If you still need Jack, let me know."

Then James practically shooed us out the door, following right behind us moments later.

I was standing on the sidewalk right outside the door when she said, "I'll help."

The problem was that I didn't want her to help.

I didn't want her anywhere near anything related to Layton Trammel.

What I couldn't do was tell her no, especially not when she gave me those eyes that she was currently giving me.

"Fuck," I muttered.

Something inside of me shifted, and I nodded once. "Give me your number and we'll…"

"You don't need her number. Get her email."

Tegan the slime bag.

I rolled my eyes.

"You think you can give us a minute? We're talking business," I said.

Tegan's eyes narrowed.

"A minute, Tegan," Janie repeated, sounding nearly hostile.

My lips twitched at the anger I could read in Tegan's eyes.

"This isn't funny."

I returned my eyes to Janie.

"What isn't funny?" I hedged.

I know I hadn't been laughing. Hell, I hadn't even betrayed a smile.

There was no way she knew that I found it all amusing.

"I can see the laughter in your eyes. I know you, Rafe."

My eyes narrowed. "Do you?"

Her mouth opened and then closed.

She didn't say a word.

"Why won't anyone tell me anything?" I asked.

Janie shrugged. "How's your *fiancé*?"

The word 'fiancé' was asked so scornfully that I nearly laughed.

I almost said, 'What fiancé?' but was able to catch myself in time.

"Elspeth is fine," I answered instead. "As I answered on the way in."

Janie looked like she swallowed a bug.

"So, you need help?"

She wasn't going to answer.

Which made me angry.

"I don't understand why no one will tell me anything," I finally said, raising my voice and waving my hands. "I just want answers!"

And I wanted those answers yesterday.

The not knowing what was going on thing was fucking frustrating.

And there was no telling if I'd get my memory back if they said something, but the least they could do was humor me.

I wanted to know my life.

It was fucking horrible living a life that I felt like a visitor in.

Tegan was at her side a moment later, scowling at me and wrapping one hand around her upper arm.

Janie didn't bother to even look at him. She kept her eyes solely on me.

"Rafe," she looked momentarily scared. "I…do you have a wedding date set yet?"

Why did she keep going back to that?

No, I didn't have a wedding date.

There wouldn't be a wedding, yet she didn't need to know that.

The more people who knew my true intentions, the more people who could possibly screw it up.

I shrugged in answer. "I don't know."

"You don't know…" Janie drawled.

My lips twitched at her obvious anger.

Goddammit, I wished I could remember!

This woman, she was making me feel things that I hadn't felt in a really long time. Since before my father was outed, and I learned he was a bigger piece of shit than I originally thought.

Was this what happiness felt like?

Seeing her getting all riled up over a woman—one I didn't even like, let alone plan on marrying—was just downright amusing. Making me tease her more than I probably should have.

Which obviously was the wrong thing to do considering what happened next.

"What do you know, Rafe?" she snapped.

All amusement fled.

"I don't know much of anything, Janie," I replied, suddenly angry. "Nobody will tell me a goddamn thing. Not one single fuckin thing, and it's irritating as fuck. Do you have anything you want to tell me?"

I'd asked her already, and again, like before, she pressed her lips together.

"Janie?" Tegan started.

Janie turned, and then Tegan dropped down to one knee.

It was exactly like in the movies.

Janie looked flabbergasted that Tegan was asking, and she looked around to see who was watching.

Apparently, it wasn't just me who got a front row seat.

It was her father, her stepmother, and a few other men and women who were doing various things outside.

All of them were solely focused on us—and Janie.

Apparently, my raising my voice had caused them to all stop what they were doing and stare.

Which then made them spectators of a show that they had no clue was about to happen.

And, out of all of this, I focused my attention on Tegan.

I'd never been a violent person when it wasn't warranted.

But, when it was warranted, I held no prisoners.

This Tegan kid was all of twenty-eight at most, and his eyes were so jealous of me that I wanted to punch him.

He didn't have anything on me.

This thing that I felt for Janie far outweighed anything that he'd ever feel, yet he was ruining everything.

I wanted to regain my memory because I was sure if I had, some of these things that I was feeling would be answered.

Did we have something together? Did she feel the same thing that I felt? Why didn't she answer any of my questions?

And the main reason I wasn't doing anything was because I was immersed in a dangerous game that I didn't want her anywhere near.

Yet, I had asked for her help because I was stupid. I wanted to be closer to her, and if I had to let her into my investigation of a man who I despised to accomplish that, I would.

Was it a good idea? No.

Was I going to do it anyway? Yes.

"Will you marry me, Janie?" Tegan asked finally.

Janie turned her eyes to me, looking, waiting for something that I didn't understand.

Was she wanting me to tell her not to do it? Because I'd tell her.

But I felt like she was searching for more. Trying to get me to do something, but I had no clue what it was.

***

Janie

Tell me you remember me. Tell me that this was all just a sick joke and that you're the only one for me. Tell Tegan to take a hike.

Something.

Anything.

Rafe!

I studied him, hoped that he would say something, anything, a single word...that would be all it took.

Yet he didn't say anything.

He just stared, impassively, as he watched me watch him.

I felt Tegan move, and I turned to him.

"You're killing me," he replied, a smile on his lips.

I swallowed, glanced once more at Rafe, and then turned back to Tegan.

"Yes."

CHAPTER 12

Cobweb cooter.
-Things you don't want to hear about on your wedding day

Janie

Two months later
The day before the wedding

My father was staring at me from across the dinner table.

"What?"

"You're sure about this?" he asked.

I looked away.

I wasn't sure about anything.

Not one single thing.

Well, that was a lie.

I was sure of one thing.

I kept holding out hope that Rafe would stop me, but he hadn't.

I'd seen him multiple times since the day that Tegan had proposed and still nothing.

He didn't remember me, I couldn't tell him who we were to each other, and every time he stared at me like he didn't know me, my heart would break just a little more.

I knew I was making a mistake with Tegan, but honestly, I kept hoping that Rafe would suddenly remember everything we had and stop me.

Yet he didn't.

And tomorrow I was supposed to be marrying a man that I didn't love.

It was stupid, childish, and the worst decision of my life.

Yet I kept wishing that Rafe would come around. That he'd remember. But it never freaking happened.

And it sucked.

I was so stupid.

But I wouldn't give up hope. I wouldn't.

My last-ditch effort had been sending him a freakin' invitation to the wedding…and then he'd RSVP'd. For two.

Him and his plus one—his fiancé.

Which led to now.

Tomorrow was the wedding.

In twelve short hours, I would be marrying a man that I didn't love.

I would be forever attached to someone because I kept thinking that if Rafe knew that I was marrying another man, surely his male instincts would kick in and he'd remember that he wanted me.

Remember that I was the only woman for him.

"Janie."

I looked up to find my father staring at me like he knew the dilemma that was currently working its way through my mind.

"Yeah?" I croaked.

"If you have even an inkling of a doubt, you should stop this," he stated.

I looked down at the table.

My problem was that if I couldn't have Rafe, I didn't see why I would ever want anybody else.

Anybody would always be second best to him.

Always.

So, what did it matter who I married when that person wasn't ever going to be Rafe?

"What are you ordering?" I changed the subject.

I'd never felt like I was making a terrible decision—at least truly—until that very second when I saw my father's face fall and fill with disappointment.

***

James
"Who gives this woman?" the preacher called, looking directly at me.

I looked over at my wife, Shiloh, and stared.

She shook her head, telling me without words not to put voice to the concerns that were rolling through me.

This all had happened too fast.

She wasn't supposed to grow up this fast. She wasn't supposed to get married. She wasn't supposed to marry someone that I didn't approve of. She wasn't supposed to leave me!

Which would be what she was doing.

Janie didn't know that her husband and I despised each other. She didn't know that by marrying him, she was betraying me.

And I would forever put that mask on each time he walked in the room if it made her happy.

The thing was, I wasn't sure that she was happy.

Not with the way her eyes kept straying to the twelfth row, fourth seat in. Not with the way she kept her eyes on me more than she did her husband.

Not with the way this whole entire thing just felt like the worst possible idea in the universe.

"I do," I said softly.

So softly, in fact, that the preacher had to strain to hear what I was saying.

Tegan reached to take Janie's hand, and it took everything I had inside of me to let her go.

Janie frowned as she stared at me with worry in her eyes, causing me to take a deep breath and take a step back.

Taking another breath, I turned on my heels and walked to my chair, not looking up again until it was done.

***

Rafe

My gut felt like I had a lead balloon in it as I stared at Janie.

She had on a white dress—something I wouldn't have expected from her. It wasn't her style.

The dress was beautiful, yes, but she didn't look the least bit comfortable in it. Nor did she look happy to be marrying the man at her side.

The man who looked as if he was holding onto her for dear life.

His hand was clenched around hers, and I could see her skin bunched up from where he'd gripped her hand so hard.

Janie looked at me twice, and each time she did my body felt like she was jerking at invisible strings attached to my heart.

She wanted me to do something. She was waiting.

I had a feeling, at least.

Each time I contemplated standing up. Each time I had to talk myself down.

She was marrying a cop. She was better off where she was going to be.

She'd have the picket fence, two-story house with the dog and the kids.

She'd have everything she ever wanted. Everything that I couldn't offer her.

What did I have to offer that Tegan didn't? Nothing, that's what.

I had a car and a bike that were paid for. I had a few other safe houses that I never lived in—one that I hadn't even been to in well over a year. Then there was my job—a job that continuously put me into dangerous situations.

I did stuff to some people that didn't like me meddling in their business.

And mostly, I was just making fucking excuses.

It all boiled down to the fact that I was goddamn pissed.

I was pissed that she was hiding something from me. I was pissed that nobody would tell me what was going on and why I felt this connection with her.

I was upset that she was treating me like everybody else.

I knew we had something, yet I felt betrayed that she was hiding it.

My stomach roiled when I heard the preacher ask, "Are there any objections?"

I got up calmly, walked down the aisle, and straight out of the church, not once looking back.

***

Janie

It took one single look at him, seeing the betrayal in his eyes directed at me, that made me realize that Rafe was gone out of my life for good.

CHAPTER 13

Author note: I, Lani Lynn Vale, solemnly swear that there is NO CHEATING in this book...but looks are deceiving. So hang with me.

Rafe

A door banged shut one down the hall from mine, and I automatically looked up.

Then I froze.

Son. Of. A. *bitch*.

Seriously, could my life get any worse?

That, I thought, as I walked out of the wedding a few hours ago was before I heard Elspeth hastily clopping along behind me.

Now, I realized, that life could, in fact, get worse.

How, you ask?

By the woman that you couldn't stop thinking about getting a hotel room not just in the same hotel as you, but also on the same floor. Right next fucking door to your own.

That would've blown big donkey balls if I'd had to hear them all night.

I would have to leave.

I couldn't be on the same floor right next door to her.

I just couldn't.

I took a step in her direction, then stopped myself.

Another step.

Two.

Three.

This was the worst idea I'd ever had. The worst.

Elspeth was in the hotel room that I'd rented for the night. *Where was I?*

Well, I was following *the* girl.

I'd seen her out of pure happenstance. I'd been in the hallway trying to get a hold of my sister. There had to be a reason that girl getting married to someone else hurt so fucking bad. Yet, again, my sister admitted that she knew nothing about 'this Janie girl' and to stop calling and asking the same question over and over.

And she was still in her goddamn wedding dress.

The only thing that had changed between then and now was the hair. It wasn't up in the complicated bun that I'd hated. Now it was down around her face, cascading down her shoulders to about mid back. God, with her hair down? She was by far the most beautiful woman I'd ever seen.

And the moment I saw her my gut clenched.

Fuck.

I took her in all over again, just as I'd done when she'd walked down the aisle, then stood next to that schmuck who was ruining my life for reasons I didn't understand.

Her dress was a little more wrinkled than when she was standing at the altar, almost as if she'd been sitting down with it scrunched up around her waist.

The tiara that'd been in her hair was gone, and the shoes were as well. Her makeup was scrubbed off, and her eyes looked tired.

The ice bucket looked exceptionally large in her hands, making me realize that she was a small woman. I'd had my ice bucket in my hands earlier in order to read the words on it and had thought it small. But in her hands? No. It was big.

Which would mean she'd be small in my hands, too.

Her hips were round, her breasts perfect, and those lips!

The door slammed to the vending room, and I moved.

I couldn't tell you why. It was a compulsion. Something my body was practically screaming that I had to talk to her. I had to ask her why.

Why the hell I felt like I was drowning with no fucking way to ever tread water again.

Like my legs had chains that weighed me down.

Each time I looked at Elspeth, I felt fucking sick to my stomach. But when I looked at Janie? I felt like I could breathe again. At least until today, when I'd watched walk down the aisle to another man.

Ever since walking out? I couldn't catch my breath. I just knew something was wrong. I'd missed something. Something pivotal, and it was eating me alive.

I pushed through the door of the vending machine room and came to a stop. She was standing there, ice bucket in hand, staring at the wall.

My stomach clenched, and I took a step forward, letting the door close behind me. The moment the soft click sounded in the room, she turned.

And when her eyes lit on me, her mouth fell open and her eyes welled with tears.

"Rafe," she breathed.

Why couldn't I fucking remember?

I knew deep in my heart that this woman meant something to me, but I couldn't figure out why. Nobody would fucking tell me why.

I knew that my memory was affected. But I remembered everything else. Everything but her or anything that had happened in the last six months.

This woman meant something to me. She meant something big to me, and I *would* figure out why.

I took a menacing step forward and she froze, her eyes rounding and her mouth parting slightly.

"Tell me why my fucking heart hurts," I ordered.

Janie swallowed, the delicate muscles or her throat working.

"I…" she started, but then stopped. "I can't."

"Why?" I took another step forward.

"Because you're engaged."

Why did that matter?

"What does that have to do with why my heart hurts?" I took another step forward.

She licked her lips, and my patience snapped.

I was lurching forward and reaching for her in the next heartbeat.

She didn't resist me. She didn't fight. Didn't scream and tell me no.

The minute my mouth was close enough, I took her into my arms and slammed my lips onto hers.

The minute I did, she started to struggle. Not to get away, though, but to get closer.

"I don't care anymore," I growled, pulling away from her lips only slightly. "You're mine."

Then there was no more time for talking.

She went crazy, biting, licking and sucking. Her teeth bit into my lower lip, causing my hips to jerk. Her fingernails dug into my shoulders. Her gasp stole my breath.

I'd give her every single minuscule drop of oxygen from my lungs if it meant this moment never ended.

I needed her with a ferocity that was scary.

My hands went to her lower hips and I started to yank up the multiple layers of her wedding dress.

There were seven layers. Count those. Seven fucking layers. Each one more light and slippery than the one before.

But I didn't give up. Not that I thought I ever could.

I knew this was bad. This went against every fucking moral code I had. Every single one of them.

I had a fake fiancée that I was 'supposed' to care about in my room. I assumed she had her brand-new husband in hers.

Yet, neither one of us cared.

"Tell me," I ordered.

She shut me up with a kiss.

I finished yanking up her layers and fisted the panties covering her lush ass. With a sharp tug, they were gone. In shreds at her feet.

The minute that scrap of fabric hit the floor, she was against me. My hands went to her ass, and I growled into her ear.

"Pull my cock out of my jeans," I ordered.

She didn't waste time.

She struggled with all the fucking material around her waist, but she wouldn't be deterred.

Thirty seconds after my order was issued, she had my cock free, and I was slamming into her.

Everything about that feeling was right. Her smell. The way she fisted around my cock. The tightness. The slippery mess we were making. The way my balls pressed perfectly against her ass.

Every. Single. Fucking. Thing.

And, moments after that thought occurred to me, my memory returned with a vengeance.

Everything came back to me in a rush. Everything.

Our years we spent playing cat and mouse. The last nine months. Our first kiss outside her gate. The first time I felt myself inside of her. The way I came so hard I thought I'd died. Then began the betrayal.

Me losing my memory. Elspeth saying she was my fiancée when she most certainly wasn't. And then Janie moving on when she found out—even though they were lies. Big fat fucking lies.

Janie finding someone. Janie moving on despite her obvious love for me.

And her not saying a goddamn word about us.

My kind hand turned punishing. My anger at her. At the situation. At Elspeth and at her stupid fucking husband.

***

Janie

"Why?" he grated out. "Why would you lie? To me?"

And, just as suddenly as he'd been there, he was gone.

I had his release and mine dripping down my leg, and I couldn't get my head on straight.

But one thing I was absolutely sure of. This wasn't the end. He knew something. Had figured something out. I could see it in his eyes, and I would never make the same mistake twice.

Today, just now, something happened. He became mine, and I

became his. And there was nothing either one of us could do about it.

CHAPTER 14

I like when you laugh. Your tits jiggle. Giggle Jiggle Tits.
-Janie to Kayla

Janie

"You have two seconds to get the fuck out of my hotel room before I throw you out myself," I heard Rafe's voice raise on the other side of the door.

Lucky for me the door hadn't closed all the way, and as I pushed through it moments later, I realized that Rafe had done that on purpose.

I found out why when the door opened, and he pointed at me with his finger, though he wasn't actually looking at me.

"Get out. Now," Rafe repeated.

I saw Elspeth standing there looking upset. "But why?"

She hadn't seen me yet, and before she could, I backed away and hurried toward my own door.

My door was actually connected to his suite, meaning if I went into my own room, I'd be able to hear everything that they were saying. Especially with the way their voices were raised.

I slid my key card into the slot and threw the door open to my room, hurrying to the door that separated my suite from Rafe's.

How in the hell we'd gotten two rooms directly next to each other, I did not know. But I thanked God that we did.

"Out. Now," Rafe repeated.

Moments later, I heard the door slam, and Rafe start pacing.

I bit my lip and scooched closer to the door, pressing my ear to it.

Then he started talking, I assume, to someone on the phone.

"I hope you know that you just fucked me over so spectacularly that I don't think I can ever forgive you," Rafe said. "If there was one thing in this world that you could have done in this whole nightmare to screw me over, not telling me about her was it. I've wasted months. Months, Raven. You've had so many chances to tell me that I can't even begin to count, yet you kept quiet. Goodbye."

Then I heard something hard hit the floor next to the door, and I realized he'd thrown his phone.

I hurried to the door of my room, peeked through the peephole, and grinned.

Elspeth was pulling her suitcase behind her, angrily looking over her shoulder as she did.

Her glare at the door made it clear that she was pissed.

I waited until the elevator doors closed on her before I opened my own door and headed out.

My hand was hovering over the wood of his door when I came to my senses.

This wasn't a good idea. Not at all.

He may have remembered, but I was a freakin' mess.

I'd left...

"I shouldn't have done that."

I startled and looked up, finding the door open.

When had he opened it, and how had he done it without making any noise?

"Uhhh," I hesitated. "You shouldn't have done what?"

"Told her to leave."

"Why?"

And why the hell was my heart hurting?

"Because I had a job going, and I need her exactly where I had her," he answered. "If she's not there, she'll stop informing on the man I have you keeping a cyber eye on, and this case will slip through my fingers. I'm so fucking close I can taste it, but I couldn't stand her lies anymore."

"What lies?" I breathed.

I'd get to the job part of it later.

"The lie that she told the day at the hospital when I couldn't fucking remember anything to tell her differently," he said, his eyes on me.

"And what was that?" I breathed, hope filling my voice. Not to mention my heart.

"Her being my fiancée," he answered instantly. "She was never anything more to me than what she was, which was a means to get in with and watch her father."

"Rafe…" I whispered.

"She's not my fiancée," he said moments later. "She never has been, and she never will be. The most we've ever done—at least before I lost my memories—was kiss."

My stomach bottomed out.

"What did you do after?"

I didn't want to know.

I really didn't.

But I had to know. I had to know so we could put this behind us.

His eyes stayed steady on me, then a door opened down the hall behind us.

He yanked me into his hotel room and slammed the door shut, causing me to gasp in surprise at the suddenness of his movements.

Rafe's eyes stayed steady on me as he pushed me up against the door.

"Wouldn't want that slime bag husband of yours interrupting us," he growled, suddenly very mad.

I opened my mouth to explain, but he stopped me.

"You should've told me," he whispered. "You should've stayed strong. You should've waited. You should've believed in me."

"I…"

"You didn't," he hissed. "You didn't believe in me. Nobody ever does."

I narrowed my eyes, again opening my mouth to say something, but he stopped me again before I could.

"I don't want to hear it."

I gritted my teeth.

"She lied about being my fiancée," he said. "Then you lied by not telling me everything. By letting me believe that we didn't have anything. Everybody lied. Trace. Your father. Sam. My sister. Everybody else, I would've been okay with. What I'm not okay with is you not telling me the truth, and then going and getting yourself hitched. I think, out of everything that's happened to me, that hurts the worst."

Before he could say another word, I pushed him away from me as hard as I could, anger making my blood simmer.

"I didn't get married," I growled. "I hoped, by me going through it all, that you'd remember. That you'd remember leaving me behind. But you didn't. And I got desperate, okay? I got desperate, and I wanted you to remember. I wanted you back in my life. I wanted you to be there, and that was the only way I could do it under the circumstances."

"What circumstances?" he hissed.

"You know," I urged. "I know. You know. Everybody knows."

"Humor me." He crossed his arms over his chest. "What does everybody know?"

I opened my mouth to tell him, the devastation clear in my voice as well as the pain in my chest, but the pounding in the hallway temporarily halted what I was about to say.

"What…"

"Janie, open the door!"

CHAPTER 15

Females don't want much. Except your time, attention, money, bank account information, all of your sweatshirts…I forgot where I was going with this.
-Rafe to Janie

Rafe

A smile started to lift the corner of one lip.

"Janie!" Tegan, the slime bag, screamed. "I know you're in there, and we're going to talk about this!"

Janie sighed and covered her face with her hands.

My smile went full-blown.

"I've been waiting three months to do this…" I breathed.

Then I let go of her, pushed her slightly to the side, and opened the door.

Janie grabbed onto my hand, but she wasn't going to stop me.

This was about to go down.

I'd been waiting for this for a long time, and I couldn't wait anymore.

Knowing that he was nothing to Janie, and probably never had been, it was time.

It was time for Tegan the Ass Hat to know what he was messing with.

"Rafe," she hissed, giving one more yank to get my attention. "Please don't do this."

I pulled away from her hold and turned before she could jump on my back. Something I knew almost instinctively that she was going to try to do.

I caught her in my arms when she went to leap and moved until we were in the doorway, my back the only thing that was visible to the rest of the hallway.

"Listen to me," I whispered, eyes locked on hers. "I had to go through three fucking months of seeing him with you. Two of those months knowing that you were about to marry him. You sent me a goddamn invitation to your wedding. I. Deserve. This."

Janie's lips thinned.

"I won't hurt him," I promised. "Much."

She sagged. "Okay."

I winked at her, pressed a hot kiss to her mouth, and then urged her to go to her feet. Which she did after a slight moment of hesitation.

I turned, leaving her there, and moved out into the hallway where Tegan was slowly picking up steam. Now he was pounding on the door, and he looked quite a bit more disheveled than he did a few hours ago.

"Yo," I called loudly enough for Tegan to hear. "Stop."

Tegan turned, eyes narrowing on me, and then bared his teeth. "You."

"Me," I nodded. "What are you doing here?"

"The lady at the front desk said my fiancé was here," he snarled. "And she's not answering."

Then his eyes went to the woman who I could feel at my back, and his eyes narrowed even more.

"You lying whore."

You know that little lie I told a few seconds ago, promising Janie that I wouldn't hurt him… much?

Yeah, that was a big fat lie.

Janie, realizing that what Tegan had just said set me off, hooked her hand into my pants and tugged.

I stayed where I was, barely, and growled. "You will not address her as anything other than her goddamn name. Do you understand me?"

Tegan laughed, and that was when I saw that he had a half-empty bottle of some sort of liquor in his back pocket.

He pulled it out and took a swig, his eyes staying on the woman behind me, and not on me.

Which was his mistake.

I curled my arm backward and wrapped my fingers around Janie's wrist.

"Let go, honey," I said softly. "I don't want to hurt you."

"Oh, that's just rich," Tegan said. "All this time while she'd been seeing me, she's been fucking you? I guess I should've known that she was a slut. She dresses like one. My mother told me that, but I refused to listen."

"Your mother told you that Janie was a slut," I said softly. "And you didn't listen to her?"

"Have you seen her?" Tegan gestured to me, and Janie in return, with his bottle, causing the liquid inside to slosh. "I hit the jackpot with her. And the icing on the cake was that it would piss her father off, too. Win win."

My mouth opened to contradict that statement when Janie pushed past me. I caught her around the hip with one arm and pulled her back into my chest.

"What are you talking about, it pissing my father off?" she asked. "My father wasn't upset about us getting married."

Her 'much' was said under her breath, but I was close enough to hear it. Which caused me to grin.

That grin quickly fell away moments later when Tegan started to laugh.

"Daddy didn't tell you that I investigated him?" Tegan jeered. "I almost pinned it on him, too, but those friends of his helped."

Janie looked confused, and I took pity on her before she could try to extract any more convoluted information from a scorned, drunk man.

"Your father was put under IA—internal affairs—investigation because of a shooting he was involved in last year. Tegan was the IA investigator put in charge of your father's case. Your father did nothing wrong, but Tegan was determined to find something. He made your father's life a living hell for almost four months while he tried to pin something—anything—on him," I whispered into her ear so only she could hear.

That's when Janie went deathly still.

"You tried to send my father to jail?" Janie asked Tegan carefully.

Tegan thought now was the time to smile.

He was so fucking stupid.

He knew nothing at all about women if he thought that was going to go over well.

It would be like lighting a cat's tail on fire in the middle of a burn ban.

Everything was about to light up in flames, Tegan just didn't know it yet.

No, he was too busy gloating about his inner victory to realize that he was in water up to his throat.

I let her go. "Can you rescind your request?"

She looked over at me, then nodded once.

"I'll make it hurt, honey. Don't you worry."

Then I walked up to Tegan and took a swing.

Tegan fell to the ground like a log, his back, legs, head and feet all hitting at once.

He hit the floor with a sickening thud and then didn't move.

His eyes were closed, and the bottle of whiskey in his hand steadily leaked out onto the carpet until the only thing left was the last little bit that couldn't make its way over the lip.

I breathed out and glared. "Least you could've done was take more than one punch."

The little shit didn't answer.

"I guess you don't need our company," James' voice came from behind me.

That's when I looked over my shoulder to see not just Janie, but her father. As well as Max, Sam, Trace, Jack, Gabe, and Elliott.

All of them were staring at me—at least the men—with understanding dawning.

Janie looked like she wanted to throttle me.

I grinned at her expression, causing her eyes to narrow even more.

"This is so not funny," she said stubbornly.

"Actually," Elliott added. "It really is. Did you see what he did to him? I think I need to learn that move."

I turned my eyes back to Tegan, who still hadn't moved.

"Elliott," Janie said tiredly. "He punched him. You already know how to do that."

"Yeah," Elliott agreed. "But mine always get back up. I think it's because everyone else has bigger hands. Mine are big, but they're not *big*. You know?"

I couldn't help it. I looked down at my hands.

Then Elliott started to laugh.

"We'll see y'all later," James muttered.

"Wait," Janie said, causing me to turn and watch them retreat.

None of them stopped.

"Wait!" Janie repeated, this time on a yell. "At least take him with you!"

I snorted when Max turned back, brushed past Janie and then me, and reached down to hook Tegan around the jacket collar.

"Are you sure you want them to be alone with a man that just called you a slut?" I asked carefully.

I mean, I was all for it. But Janie was a soft soul. It'd hurt her if she found out later that she was responsible for Tegan's untimely demise.

"Oh," she breathed. "Dad, wait!"

"Hurry up!" Elliott hissed.

Max drug the little prick the rest of the way into the elevator just as Elliott was busy pressing buttons.

I couldn't help it.

I laughed.

Seeing all those men crammed into that elevator with a man at their feet as the last one in urgently tried to get the doors to close was quite comical.

Janie, however, didn't find any of it as hilarious as I did.

Which she informed me of as she slammed her way into her hotel room, and not mine, moments later.

I followed her, easily slipping in my universal key card—which I'd obtained the last time I'd stayed in this hotel—and walked right in.

I found her with her dressed tossed up as she tried to shimmy out of it.

I walked up behind her and helped her, lingering a little longer than was necessary on a few sets of buttons close to her ass.

"You're not helping," I heard her grit through clenched teeth.

I grinned—something I'd done more in the last half hour than I'd done in the last three months—and growled out a, "Turn around."

She did, clutching the loosening dress to her chest.

"I don't like this dress," I said to her, trailing my fingers along her chest.

It was bare. Not a necklace or a skin imperfection dotted the line of her neck, and that bothered me.

I wanted to mark her as mine in some way, and I wanted every man in the world to know it.

"I don't like it either," she admitted. "I got it at a discount place in Tyler. It was on sale for ninety-nine dollars."

I snorted. "The next one—the one you wear for me—is going to cost fifty times that."

Her mouth fell open, and she forgot that she was holding up her dress, which worked for me.

"T-the next one?" she whispered, her eyes on me.

I nodded. "The one where you and I walk out man and wife. The one where you don't fucking leave me at the altar, and the one where I make sure that you'll forever be mine."

"But Rafe," she hesitated. "We don't really know each other all that well."

I winked. "I'll give you a couple of months to get to know me. Then you can announce to your family that you're engaged."

"Rafe, that's not how this works," she whispered.

I trailed my finger down her side, lightly touching just the tip of my fingernail against her delicate skin, and snorted.

"This is how it works in Raphael Luis's world. Soon, you'll be Mrs. Raphael Luis. Soon, you'll be mine. And I'll make you forget that you were anything before me."

She started to laugh then, momentarily distracting me from what I was about to do.

I looked at her with a raised brow. "What?"

"I don't think you understand," she teased.

"Understand what?" I questioned.

"The part of how I've never been anybody but yours. From the time I was twelve and I first met you, you had my heart. The only time you didn't have it was when you forgot about me. But even then, you had it. You just didn't know it."

Grinning at the thought of her always being mine, I placed a single kiss on the inside of her knees.

"Rafe," she breathed.

I looked up from where I was down on my knee and raised a brow at her. "Yeah?"

"Can you do it harder this time?"

I couldn't help it.

I grinned.

"Yeah," I agreed. "I think I can handle that."

***

"So how are you going to fix this?" she whispered against my chest two hours later.

We'd left the hotel since that would be the first place Tegan would think to look when he finally came to. Not that I thought Janie's father would be letting him go anytime soon. Maybe a few days. If he was lucky.

"I don't know," I admitted. "But I'll figure it out."

And I would.

Right after I got out of bed.

"Ok, what are *we* going to do?" she pushed, poking me.

I sat up in the bed and leaned against the headboard, knowing this wasn't going to get pushed under the rug. At least, she wouldn't let me get away with it.

"What are we going to do?" I grinned.

She flushed. "You already told me you didn't want to get into it completely. You wanted me to stay out of sight from Layton. Which I will. But there's no reason I can't stay behind the scenes. Keep doing what I'm doing…"

I immediately shook my head. "I'd agree with you if I didn't know Layton. You're good, I'll give you that. But Layton will have someone just as good."

Her eyes narrowed. "Is whatever he's doing really bad?"

I pursued my lips. "I don't know."

I had a lot of theories, but none of them were substantiated.

"What do you suspect?" She caught on to my hesitation.

I sighed. "I suspect, based on Dante's thing, that he's involved in the military thefts. I was close to something before my accident. Ever since, I've been an outsider. They discuss nothing around me. Even Elspeth wasn't helping me anymore. Which is why I'm not too upset about losing that in."

She sighed. "You'll tell me if you need help?"

I leaned over in the bed and pulled her toward me. "You will be the first to know."

And as she fell asleep in my arms, I knew that I'd do everything in my power not to need her. I had a feeling that this was about to go very, very bad.

CHAPTER 16

I'm not a glass half-full kind of person. I'm more of a 'where the fuck did I put my glass' kind of person.
-Janie's secret thoughts

Janie

The first hurdle was over.

Rafe remembered.

Everything.

It hurt, and it healed all at the same time.

I wanted him to remember me. I didn't like how it felt when he didn't.

Like what we'd shared had all been a lie.

And now that I knew that what he had with Elspeth was also fake, well that was just the incentive I needed.

I had to talk to my dad.

Which was why I was up at five thirty in the morning with my rifle in hand, and my dogs at my feet, waiting beside his truck for him to come outside.

He did moments later, stopping a few feet outside of his front door to stare at me.

"You're up early."

I shrugged.

I wasn't a morning person.

I especially wasn't a morning person when I spent the majority of the previous day not sleeping. And when I say, 'not sleeping,' I mean I did some intense cardio with very little rest in between sessions.

And Rafe, my broodingly sexy man, acted like this was just a walk in the park for him.

He'd been up over an hour and a half ago and had escorted me to my front gate before the sun even came up. He'd even had to go as far as to carry me out since I couldn't seem to keep my eyes open.

After letting my dogs out of Kayla's house, I walked to my own and downed two cups of black coffee before I even began to feel remotely human.

Which led to now.

"I'm up early," I agreed. "I wanted to come with you."

Dad didn't even blink an eye at me coming with him.

I'd done it a lot when we were younger. Not so much lately seeing as I'd learned the value of sleeping in.

He walked around his truck and opened my door for me. Before I could hop in, though, my dogs leaped and made their way to the back seat where they sat down nicely.

"At least they are considerate," Dad muttered.

I agreed.

My dogs might be a pain in the ass sometimes, but they were considerate. They were also sweet, and I loved them. Rafe loved them, too, unlike Tegan.

"Why didn't you tell me that you had a problem with Tegan?" I questioned, looking at my father.

He gestured to the truck, and I got inside.

He slammed it closed and didn't answer me until we were well on our way.

"Who am I to question who my daughter marries?" he asked.

I gave him a look.

"My prom date you decided needed a lesson in putting on a condom. You made him practice it on a banana five times before you let him out of the house. The moment we got to prom, he left me and didn't return until five minutes before eleven. He picked me up, dropped me off, and then left to go out and party with people who he knew weren't going to have him killed later on for hurting them," I drawled.

My dad's mouth quirked up. "The kid was a wiener."

I had no doubts about that.

I hadn't liked him, and honestly, he was just a boy who was taking me on a date to the prom.

Personally, I would have much preferred it if Rafe took me, but it would've looked quite odd if that had happened.

Not to mention that my dad would have most certainly put a stop to that.

Now…well, I wanted to know what it was that was keeping him from telling me everything about Tegan.

I would have wanted to know.

I would've stopped it moments after finding out had I known.

"I made myself a promise when you were younger that if you were dead set on doing something, I wouldn't get in your way. I wouldn't try to persuade you from taking a different road, and I definitely wouldn't stop you if you were bound and determined to make it happen," he said into the quiet cab. "Did it kill me that you were marrying a man I disliked? Yes. But Tegan wasn't a bad guy. He was just too power hungry when it came to his job. He would've provided for you. I'd watched the two of you together, and he made you laugh. And, honestly?"

"I always want honest, Dad," I teased.

Even if it hurt.

"Tegan was just trying to make a name for himself," he started. "I disliked him. I wasn't sure if that was due to him being a douche bag at work, or because I hated him with *you*. So, to keep my emotions from getting the better of me, I chose not to tell you anything. I wanted you to make your own informed decision. And if you thought he was bad, you would've stopped it. I trust your judgment. And, eventually, I would've gotten over it."

I pursed my lips.

Dammit, I hated when he treated me like an adult!

"Sometimes, Daddy, I want you to tell me when I'm doing something you don't like," I pointed out. "You would've had to have him at every family dinner, reunion, school function. He would've been there forever."

He winked. "If it'd have been too painful, I would've told you so." He shuddered then. "But I didn't think about him being there for Christmas dinner and shit. I would've hated to ask him how he liked his eggs."

I sighed and rolled my eyes.

"I guess now's a good time to tell you what I know."

He hummed his agreement, and I buckled down and told my father everything that Rafe said I could safely share.

Rafe hadn't spared a single detail of his investigation, but he also trusted me with it all. He knew I wouldn't react badly…unlike my father who would be very interested in the case because of his time in the military.

"So, Elspeth is just part of his investigation?"

"Yeah," I confirmed. "She pulled a 'While You Were Sleeping' on him and acted like they were engaged. He didn't know any different, so he didn't contradict her."

"How did she know he was there?"

That had been a question on my mind, too.

"We don't know," I said. "He said he'd ask her, but he didn't just burn that bridge last night, he set fire to the whole village. I'm not sure what he's going to be able to find out from her at this point."

My dad grunted and took a turn that led to the back of Free property where they'd built the indoor gun range.

"He remembers everything now?"

I nodded.

"And you're sure you want to date a forty-something-year-old man?"

I grinned. "Yeah."

He stayed quiet for a few long moments, clearly trying to decide what he should say next.

And eventually decided to just say it.

"Janie," my father hesitated. "I don't think you have any clue what you're getting yourself into here." He pursed his lips as he pulled into the parking spot directly in front of the main door, then shut the truck off. "Rafe's intense. He's pissed off all the time, and I have a feeling he might try to work some of that anger out with you."

I blinked, staring blankly at the wall.

"I know exactly what I'm getting into, Dad," I said, surprised that my father would broach any subject that had to do with sex. If the subject strayed too close to that edge, he shied away. Not that he couldn't talk about it to everyone else, it was just when it came to his kids that he got uncomfortable. My aunt Cheyenne and my mother were the ones that opened that can of worms. If I wanted to know anything at all about sex, I could talk to any number of women in the family. All of them were very open with anything pertaining to sex.

Yet, hearing my father say it to me made me quite uncomfortable. Which he could tell that I was, too.

"Just…think about it, okay?" he said softly. "Think before you act.

Don't dive before you know what's under the surface. You may not like what you find, and you might be too far in to save yourself."

I didn't reply to that, but that was due in part to the fact that he'd gotten out and slammed the door.

I got out moments later and shut my door, then headed to the back seat where my father had stashed whatever guns he was using that day.

I grinned when I saw him get his sniper rifle out.

"You normally don't do that in here," I said.

The indoor range wasn't big enough.

"I'm taking it to the back," he answered.

I nodded in understanding.

In a pinch, Dad used the gun range back behind the building because it was convenient. Any other time he used KPD's official shooting range since he had to log a certain number of hours each week to stay certified as Kilgore Police Department's sniper.

Sometimes I went with him, while others I didn't want to be there for four hours while I watched him do what he'd do.

His work was important, but there was only so much sitting in silence I could take.

Luckily, if he was shooting in the back, that meant he wasn't going to be there for hours.

First of all, it was only conducive with shorter distances, and second of all, he didn't shoot very long here.

Meaning it would be a lot more entertaining than usual.

We started out inside, him shooting his service revolver because he got unlimited ammunition for practice with it, while I shot my occasional concealed carry weapon.

I say occasional because it wasn't often that I carried it.

There was just nowhere to put it.

I didn't carry a purse, and most of the time, I lived in way too tight jeans. There was just nowhere to put it unless I wanted to wear the leggings that already had the holster sewn into it. And...I was too heavy for those. I wasn't a size three. Hell, I wasn't even a size nine or ten. I was size thirteen. I had booty and thighs for days (and sometimes weeks). I wasn't squeezing my ass into leggings designed for dainty little girls.

But, every once in a while, I wore an actual pair of pants with a belt, and when that happened, I carried. And to carry, according to my father, I had a responsibility. A responsibility to the public which included me keeping my skills sharp.

Yes, that was one of the problems with having a police officer father. You did what he wanted, and you didn't complain. He knew best, and he always would.

Even when you're a grown woman with common sense of your own.

Like I was right now.

"Finger off the trig..."

I turned my glare on my father. "Dad, if you say that one more time, I might actually throat punch you."

I placed the gun on the counter where we were shooting side-by-side and pressed the button for the target to come back to me.

I grinned when I saw the grouping.

"You know you're impressed with this," I said to him, gesturing to my target.

"You're jerking up slightly to the left."

I turned to find Rafe standing almost directly behind me, and by the looks of his amusement, he'd been standing there long enough for him to hear me threaten to throat punch my father.

I frowned at him.

"How did you know where we were?" I questioned him suspiciously.

"You said you were going to go shoot with your dad, and it was only a guess on my part from there," he answered, his eyes going to my dad.

I turned to survey him too and saw that he was unsurprised to find Rafe standing there.

"I've been telling her about her jerking problem for years now. You telling her isn't going to stop it," he said by way of hello.

Rafe shrugged. "If she doesn't want to be the best…"

I sighed. "Y'all are annoying. I'd like to see you do better."

Rafe came up to my dad's side. "May I?"

My dad shrugged and stepped out of the way, and Rafe had a gun out and aimed down range faster than I could blink.

One second it was hidden somewhere, and the next he was unloading a whole freakin' magazine in the time it took me to draw my next breath.

"Holy shit," I breathed. "You're fast."

Rafe produced another magazine from somewhere—his pocket maybe—and slammed it into the butt of his gun before the spent magazine could even hit the floor. The next ten shots came in a slower procession, but no less practiced on Rafe's part.

It went like that for two more magazines, and then Rafe placed his still smoking gun down on the counter and reached up to bring the target back.

My heart was pounding.

He'd moved so fast.

I'd seen my dad move like that, but Rafe was something else. It was different watching the man you had the hots for do it. It was as if he had a line straight to my vagina!

And God, the muscles in his forearm that bunched with each recoil from his gun—total spank bank material.

"Janie, what the hell?" my dad asked.

I swallowed and bent down to pick up the box of targets that I'd somehow knocked down in my perusal of the man that I loved.

When I stood back up and shuffled the targets into a row, my eyes lit on Rafe, who was watching me with amusement.

I mock glared at him, causing his grin to widen.

Then I looked away, not wanting to rub anything in my father's face if I could help it—and got my first good look at the target.

"You missed," I said in surprise.

"He didn't miss," my dad said. "He made it. All forty-one shots. He shot the top right there, see?"

I did see after he pointed it out.

The targets my father used were the ones that had a tiny example of the targets in the top corner, and on that smaller-scaled picture, there was an explanation of each ring's points.

All shots but one—which was at the head of the tiny little target— was dead center in the middle of the mini-target.

Holy. Shit.

"Holy crap," I said. "That's impressive as hell."

"Practice," Rafe said. "But I shot all my hollow points. I'll have to go get more. Y'all save the brass?"

Dad nodded, and Rafe went around picking up the spent brass shell casings. Once he had his hands full, he walked them over to the jug in the corner and slowly dropped them inside without another word.

My dad caught my eye, and for the first time, I saw him grinning.

"I can do that, too, you know."

I snorted. "Yeah, yeah, yeah. Go ahead and make me feel like a subpar human being, why don't you?"

Rafe came up behind me and placed his large palm on the small of my back.

"You're not a subpar human being, but before you start gloating, you should see if you really are the best one in the room," Rafe teased.

I pinched his non-existent belly fat. "Thanks for nothin'."

Rafe winked and then let me go, clearly uncomfortable with any public displays of affection with my father anywhere near around.

Not that I could blame him.

The poor guy had a huge mountain to climb when it came to my family.

They'd disliked him from the very beginning, and was over something Rafe had absolutely zero control of. I would be sure to inform my family that their shit ended when we got together.

And they would give me that.

They wanted me to be happy, and it would be very apparent to everyone in the room that he made me happy.

All they had to do was look at my googly eyes that I couldn't hide when it came to the man.

"So, Mr. McHot Pants, how do I fix my jerking problem?" I teased.

He replied in an instant.

"You're anticipating the recoil so you're bracing your hand once you've already pulled the trigger. Which then causes your hand to jerk slightly," he answered. "What I would suggest is this," then he moved behind me and showed me how he'd hold the gun.

But, when he was done explaining, he didn't move back. He stayed where he was. "Try it.

And I did. I did exactly what he showed me, with him solidly at my back.

And I shot a bullseye seven times.

I was profusely impressed.

"Not that I don't think that was cool, but you can't be standing at my back all the time. What happens if you're not here and I need to take care of business?" I looked up at him and batted my eyelashes rapidly.

He bent down and whispered in my ear. "If you need me there, I will be. As your support, your guide, or even to take that gun from your hand and do it myself. I'll be there. If I'm not, I'll get there as fast as I can. The day that I'm not will be the day that I'm dead."

Tears threatened to choke me.

I wanted to say so many things to him. Wanted him to know that I'd be those same things to him. But my dad interrupted the moment by cursing.

Then Rafe was gone from my back, but he smoothed his hand down my backside before he went, making the loss not so terrible.

I turned once I had myself under control, looking to see my dad with his hand on his chest.

"Daddy?"

Lani Lynn Vale

204

CHAPTER 17

Are nap dates a thing? I could go for a snuggle.
-Janie to Rafe

Rafe

"Jesus Christ. Would y'all get off of me? I'm fucking fine. They said it was nothing," James growled to those around him. "Get the fuck out of here!"

I kept my grin in check. Barely.

"Come on, ladies. Let's go get some food from the cafeteria," I suggested to Janie and her two sisters that wouldn't stop pestering their father.

Shiloh, James' wife, was smiling.

Janie tried to fluff James' pillows again, and he'd had enough.

"Janie, swear to God if you touch my goddamn pillow one more time..."

Time for me to step in.

"It was a gallbladder attack, y'all," I said, stepping farther into the room. "He's going to be perfectly fine. They'll probably suggest surgery to remove it, which will be superb because gallbladder attacks fucking blow."

Scout, Janie's youngest sister, snorted. "And how would you know?"

My lips twitched at her angry words. "I had my gallbladder out when I was thirty. Best feeling ever to be able to eat again. Freakin' sucked ball…sucked bad," I answered. "But it's not a death sentence. It's just a nuisance."

"Promise?"

I looked over to see the fear written all over Scout's face.

"I can't promise anything. Life is life. Sometimes it doesn't work out like you want it to. However, based on what I know, it's fairly routine. He'll probably be released within the hour barring any problems with his lab work."

Scout took a deep breath and then leaned into me. "Thank you, Rafe."

I grinned and looped my arm around her shoulder. Janie's other sister, Rebel leaned into my other side, and Janie gave me a beaming smile.

I'd passed the sister test. Sweet.

"I don't have my wallet," Janie suddenly said, turning to go back.

I caught her by the wrist, letting go of Scout. "I have a wallet."

She frowned.

"You don't have…" She started to say.

I squeezed her wrist a little tighter.

"I'm going to," I declared, leaving no room for argument.

She harrumphed, then fell into step again.

I turned back around myself and caught Scout's eye when I did.

Her happy, knowing smirk had me raising my brow.

She didn't look like Janie. She was a much slimmer girl than Janie would ever be and probably had ever been. My guess was that she was always going to be small. Tall and lanky would be a better description. But she was adorable nonetheless.

I pulled open the door to the cafeteria once we'd arrived and held it open for all three.

Janie went first, Scout second, and Rebel trailed in last.

Since Rebel lagged behind, I tugged her close like I'd done Scout moments before.

Seemed as if three out of four Allen women were not handling this very well. It was hard to see their patriarch go down when they were used to him being formidable.

Janie looked over her shoulder at me and grinned.

Seemed as if she was loving this forced family time, and secretly, I was, too.

I wanted to get to know them.

I hadn't under these circumstances, of course, but I wouldn't complain. Not when I'd wanted this for what felt like a lifetime.

I wanted Janie in my life, and Janie came with her family.

Therefore, I'd take everything that I could get.

We got up to the counter where the food was, and each girl ordered dessert first.

"I'll have two chocolate chip cookies," Scout said.

"I want a slice of that cheesecake right there," Rebel pointed at it.

"And I'd like a piece of that fudge cake you have," Janie pointed as well.

I burst out laughing, and all three of them looked at me with confusion.

"What?" Janie asked, confusion written all over her face.

My lip twitched as another laugh threatened to break free.

"Nothing." I shook my head. "Y'all are just a lot alike. It surprised me, that's all."

Janie pursed her lips but didn't comment.

"Are y'all only having dessert or are you actually eating a meal?" I questioned.

Each of them ordered a burger and fries, then all three saturated the burgers they received with so much ketchup I wasn't sure they could even taste the meat.

The fries came next where each squirted not just ketchup, but mustard, all over the tops.

I wanted to vomit.

"That's just wrong," I said upon seeing their blasphemous ways. "I don't even know if I can ever kiss you again."

Janie started to laugh, then she scooped a fry covered in that disgusting concoction into her mouth.

I vowed that I wouldn't give her another kiss at least until she brushed her teeth, and then broke that vow moments later when she offered me her lips.

I, of course, didn't hesitate to take them.

***

Janie

Later that night, I relayed my father's and my conversation prior to him arriving that morning, to Rafe who was in the bathroom.

"He's right, you know," Raphael's smooth, deep voice said from behind me, startling me with his sudden presence. "I'm terrible for you."

I spun around and stared at the man that I loved with all my heart but wouldn't give me the time of day.

At least, at one point in time.

Today, he'd proven to me that I wasn't just a passing fling.

I was something to him.

I wasn't too young or naïve any longer. I was Janie Allen, the woman who was slowly worming her way into his heart.

"I think you have no clue what I want, otherwise you'd stop trying to persuade me into thinking otherwise," I said in all seriousness.

He shook his head and walked to the kitchen table. Once there, he pulled a chair out, spun it around, and then straddled it backward.

His longish hair was wild around his head.

Since he'd come home from his 'deployment' he'd been growing it out. It was now down around his ears.

Normally I only ever saw it when it was tamed and perfectly in place.

Tonight, though, it flowed free.

Crazy brown locks flew wildly around his face, and the scar on his eye as well as the tattoo that crawled up the side of his neck almost seemed more sinister than they already were.

Jesus, the man was sex personified.

He was everything that I shouldn't want, and the one thing that I really needed all rolled into a perfect ball of badass.

I moved until I was behind him, then reached forward and ran my fingers through the unruly locks.

"It surprises me that your hair is this wild even though it's not that long," I whispered, scratching his scalp with my fingernails.

He leaned back and let his head lean against my chest.

"Spent all those years being forced to do this, or that, when it came to my hair. I'm thankful I can actually grow it out without getting reprimanded." He paused. "But I plan on getting a trim tomorrow."

"I don't know," I teased. "I kind of enjoy having something to grab hold of."

He let his head trail along my breasts, rubbing back and forth, causing my nipples to peak and harden.

I swallowed and tugged on his hair, causing him to lean his head back even more.

Then I leaned forward and kissed him upside down.

"You know," I said against his lips. "This is a definite turn from the other few times we've done this."

I pulled away slightly and let him see my eyes, and the mirth that filled them.

"You want to be in charge?" he asked.

I swallowed, then nodded. "For a little bit, anyway."

He stood up, and I let go of his head so I wouldn't break his neck, and then turned so that he was sitting in the chair normally.

"What will you have me do, mistress?"

I bit my lip. "It's not what I would have you do," I said, dropping down to my knees. "It's what I want to do to you."

He turned in his seat and I scooted between his thighs.

Then I reached for his jeans, unbuttoned them, and tugged lightly.

He caught what I was asking and lifted his hips, allowing me to pull his pants down to pool around his ankles.

I smirked up at him. "Do you ever wear underwear?"

He shrugged.

"Sometimes. When I feel like it," he answered.

I shook my head. "If I didn't wear panties, would it drive you insane?"

His eyes flared.

"You go without panties, and we're going to have problems," he countered.

"Why?" I leaned forward and pressed a kiss to his thigh.

He hissed in a breath.

"Because," he said.

I kissed the other thigh.

His legs were tan, despite it being the dead of winter, and I found that it was quite annoying how he was always so perfect.

Even his cock was perfect.

It was long, thick, and had the picture-perfect head topping it.

Seriously, penises weren't pretty. At least, I'd never found them pretty.

But Rafe's wasn't just pretty. It was everything a woman would want in a penis.

"For Christ's sake. Please, put it in your mouth already."

I snorted.

"You're not very good at this me being in charge thing, are you?" I teased.

I leaned forward and circled the tip of his cock with my tongue, flicking the underside a little more roughly than I would've if he hadn't urged me to take him.

He growled, and I felt his hands move to his thighs. I looked at those hands out of the corner of my eyes and nearly laughed at the way his fingers were white with how hard he was holding on.

"Feel okay?" I inquired.

"Yes," he gritted out. "Fucking perfect."

I'd done nothing but touch my tongue to him. What would he do when I took him in my mouth?

I pulled back, made sure to catch his eyes, and then leaned back down, this time maintaining eye contact while I took him into my mouth.

The feel of his smooth penis encased in a silky layer of steel was enough to make my thighs clench in need at the anticipation of what he would feel like when he was inside of me.

"Sweet baby Jesus," he groaned.

I would've laughed had my mouth not already been occupied.

Instead of giving him that, though, I pushed his cock so far into my throat that I started to gag.

And he started to lose control.

Over and over I pulled out just to take him back inside until I felt him finally snap.

His hands went to my hair, and his hips jerked.

"Warning."

I didn't stop.

Didn't even think about stopping.

I suctioned my mouth around the tip, pumped him with two hands, and nearly moaned when I felt the first spurt of his come hit my mouth.

"Oh, fuck," he repeated for what seemed the fifteenth time in as many minutes.

I swallowed. Then swallowed again.

And finally, when he was no longer spurting freely, I pulled back and looked up at him.

"Okay?"

He nodded, his head now leaned back, and his Adam's apple bobbing as he struggled to take in deep breaths of air.

"Think you can return the favor?" I asked, stripping my shirt over my head.

His head came up, and he nodded once. "Yeah," he croaked. "I think I can manage to return the favor."

Then he surged upward, hooked an arm behind my hips, and then threw me up on his shoulder.

Moments later he kicked off his boots, making me squeal in fear as I tipped a little too far forward for comfort, and gasped. "Rafe, seriously, put me down!"

He grunted as he kicked off his jeans, ignoring the thud of the things he still had in his pockets.

I giggled as he did and held on for the ride as he walked quickly into his room.

***

Rafe

She was so fuckin' beautiful that sometimes it was hard for me to believe that she wanted me.

Who the hell was I?

I was a nobody.

I was Raphael Luis, the piece of shit son of a man who had ruined many lives and then left me to deal with the repercussions.

A nobody.

"Rafe?"

I followed her down on the bed and went face to face with her.

"Every single fucking day—until I met you—was a struggle."

Janie's mouth fell open.

"The day you told me that you were sorry I had one ball was the day that I realized that maybe life wasn't as bad as I'd made it out to be," I told her. "I was mad at the world. Pissed off that I couldn't do what I wanted to do—which was find Layton Trammel and shove my fist down his throat in order to rip out his lungs. Then you came along, with your sarcastic mouth, and changed my life."

Janie drew in a breath.

"Not a day went by that I didn't hate what my dad had forced me to become," I continued. "Then there you were, torturing me through the years."

"I didn't torture you!" she cried out, poking me with one small finger directly in the middle of my breastbone.

I grinned. "You didn't try to seduce me with those tight jeans, and shorter than sin skirts when you were jailbait?"

"Hoo haha."

My brows rose in confusion. "Hoo haha?"

"Finding Nemo, the movie. Though, the saying was 'Shark Bait.

Hoo haha."

I snorted. "And this is another example of how we're so far apart in age. You've watched Finding Nemo. When I was a kid, we watched Saturday morning cartoons."

Janie's lips tipped up at the corners.

"If I was sixteen again, then this age gap between us would matter," she murmured, reaching up to press a kiss on my jaw. "But since I'm well over the legal age of consent, which in Texas is seventeen, you have nothing to worry about. So, you'll die before me. Big deal."

I tickled her, causing her to screech and try to pull away.

I didn't let her get so much as an inch away from me as I sat us both back up, her in my lap.

The new move pressed her ass right against my hard again cock.

She wiggled her butt and smiled unrepentantly when I squeezed the fleshy part of her ass tightly, saying without words that she needed to stop. Or else.

Janie pursed her lips but tried to remain as still as possible.

"It's not a big deal."

Her brows went up.

"Because we won't make it a big deal," I amended. "What we have is what we want. And nobody and nothing is going to change that. That's my promise to you."

"So, when someone calls you a cradle robber," she said, running the tip of one finger down my bearded jaw. "That's not going to piss you off?"

I grinned. "No."

"And when they ask if you're my daddy?"

The twinkle in her eyes would've made me laugh had I not thought she was partially serious with the question.

"Then I'll tell them only in the bedroom," I countered.

She choked and slapped me on the chest. "That's going to get us kicked out of wherever the hell we happen to be at the time."

I shook my head. "I think you'll be surprised with how tolerant everyone is of a relationship like the one we have."

"Rafe?" she whispered, leaning even closer to me.

The shift in her weight had her putting more pressure on my dick, and I pushed her off of me before she could wiggle that sumptuous ass any more against me.

"Can I?" she asked, scrambling up onto her knees the moment her ass met the mattress.

"Can you what?" I asked warily.

"Can I touch your ball. The one that is fake?"

I rolled my eyes. "You don't have to ask."

"I was thinking that was the case, but I didn't want to touch it in case it hurt, or in case you were all sensitive about it," she explained.

I leaned back on the bed and moved my hands up to my head and got comfortable.

Once she saw I was letting her do whatever she wanted, she scrambled up between my legs and poked one.

"Is it this one, or the other one?"

"Which one do you think it is?" I asked when she pressed the skin on my left one.

"They both look exactly the same," she pointed out.

"They don't feel the same," I countered.

She took one lip between her teeth and bit it lightly as she started to massage my balls. First one, then the other, until she pointed with her finger. "This one?"

I shrugged, wanting her to guess.

"It's harder. A little rounder and less squishy. What did they put in there to make it hold its shape?" she questioned.

"It's a prosthetic implant. They showed it to me when I had the implant done. It looks similar to a clear, shell-less egg. It almost feels like a hardboiled egg, if you think about it," I explained.

"It does," she agreed.

"This one is the fake one?" she asked, her fingers playing delicately over the implant.

"Yes," I said, trying to make my breathing even.

I may not actually have any feeling in that particular testicle, but the skin was still just as sensitive.

My cock was so hard it hurt, but I'd let her be curious.

She was having fun, and I was having fun watching her touch me.

My cock lay bobbing against my hairy belly, up and down. Up and down.

She was fixated on it. Her eyes watched every single movement, taking everything in, and missing nothing.

The drop of pearly white come that beaded on the tip of my cock. The way it leaned slightly to the left. Then there was the way my breathing had picked up in anticipation of having her again.

It would never get old. Not ever.

Nothing compared to having her in my arms.

"Come here," I said, holding my hand out to her. "And kiss me."

Janie's lips met mine within a half a second as she scrambled up my legs and deposited her pussy right over the top of my cock.

"We need to talk about birth control," I said, knowing that it was a mood killer, but knowing that we needed to have the talk as well.

I'd failed each time I'd had her.

A condom hadn't even crossed my mind, and I was a grown ass adult. I didn't even have youth to fall back on as an excuse for acting like I didn't know what I was doing. I did. I knew exactly what I was doing. I wanted inside her bare every single time, but what I didn't want to do was do anything without her knowing what we were doing.

"I'm on the pill," she said. "I have been for a while now."

I was thankful as well as annoyed all at once. "Why?"

Her smile was soft.

"Because I knew, if one day you decided to give me the time of day, I better be prepared."

That felt like I'd just taken a sledgehammer to the chest.

"Yeah?" I asked.

"Yeah," she confirmed.

I reached up and brought her mouth to mine as I urged her to rock her hips.

She did, coating my cock with her juices as she did.

I let her, enjoying the way she felt sliding all over my length.

"You're so wet," I growled, rolling then. "Tell me it's only for me."

I looked down into her eyes and ground my cock into her heat.

"It's only ever been you, Rafe."

I frowned.

"Just me?"

She nodded.

"You didn't..."

"I didn't have a hymen?" She guessed where I was going with my statement.

I nodded.

"Rafe," she giggled. "I think it's a fairly normal thing nowadays to have a vibrator. You weren't the first thing to go in there, but you were the first authentic, living thing."

"Hmm," I grunted. "That's cool, I guess."

"That's cool?" she teased. "That was freakin' what got me through my teen years with you around."

I let the grin overtake my lips.

"Tell me what you did," I ordered. "Better yet," I flipped onto my back. "Show me."

"I was always on my back," she whispered.

"Yeah, but you also probably had a rhythm you took," he said. "Fuck me like you fucked yourself."

Her eyes gleamed as she rolled up onto all fours and started to straddle me.

"Did you get yourself wet first, or use lube?" I questioned.

"Lube," she answered. "Seemed easier at the time."

"It is," I agreed. "I have some in the nightstand drawer."

She leaned over me, her breasts trailing across my chest, and opened the drawer.

I knew the instant she saw what was in there, too, because she froze.

"Something in there you like?"

She slammed the drawer shut, then sat up with her fingers clutched tightly around the lube.

"I don't think I'm ready for your magic drawer of wonders," she whispered, fear as well as curiosity lingering in her eyes.

"One day you will be," I added. "But for today, you just treat me like I'm your BOB at home."

"BOB?"

"Battery operated boyfriend," I amended.

She snorted. "I call it by its name. Which is a Lula. But you can call it a BOB if you want."

I reached for her hand and tugged her to me. "You're stalling."

She licked her lips, then dropped down to press a kiss to my jaw.

"You just lie there and let me make myself come," she ordered, straddling my thighs once again.

I watched as she did, my hard cock filling up the space between her parted thighs quite nicely.

Then she took the lube, clicked open the cap with one thumb, and upended it.

I didn't say a word as she did what she would.

Instead, I watched her pour way too much on me, then start slicking me up and down. She'd used so much on me that it started to slide down my shaft, past my sac, and down to the crack of my ass to the bed.

I didn't care that we were making a mess.

I only cared about the fact that she was here. That she was lubing me up.

Neither one of us said a word as she made the biggest mess in the universe.

I didn't say a word at all while she worked the lube down over my length, then parted her thighs as she brought that same hand she'd been using on me to her own pussy lips.

Once she was sufficiently coated, she threw the bottle down on the bed and scooted into place high up over my cock.

And when she sat down, easily guiding my cock into her, it took everything I had not to arch up and meet her. Or better yet, grab her by the hips and force myself into her so deep and hard that she screamed.

Either way, I would've been happy.

Then again, I wasn't unhappy, either, with the way she slowly sank down on me. I was just frustrated.

I wanted more. Harder, and faster.

But I didn't do anything to stop her.

She was the driver of this show, and I was going to stick to my word whether I wanted to die right now or not.

My eyes closed, and I was fairly sure that every single muscle in my body was straining to stay where it was.

My palms were clenched in the bedspread. My fingernails hurt because I was hanging on so hard.

Then there were my feet.

My toes were actually curled.

She placed the tip of my cock at her entrance, and my eyes flew open.

And she was smiling.

She was enjoying this.

I broke.

I couldn't do it.

Not today.

Not when this was so new.

Not when everything about her was still so new, so fresh.

I'd had her a grand total of five times.

Five.

Count those.

One. Two. Three. Four. Five.

And that wasn't enough.

It'd probably never be enough, but at least after a few decades of having her, I might begin to control myself a little better.

I saw the change come over her face. She knew I broke.

She looked victorious. As if that was what she'd been planning this entire time.

"You little bitch," I breathed.

Then I had her on her back, and my cock filling her sweet, hot pussy moments later.

Her back arched, and the cords on her neck strained, and she screamed as I filled her up.

With the amount of lube she used, everything slid all the way in.

Which was a surprise to her because normally I had to work myself in. But not today. Today, she'd been primed. Not to mention, she'd already given me a blow job, and I knew for a fact that it'd turned her on.

Speaking of that blow job, technically, I guess, that should mean that I shouldn't be close.

But I was.

I was so close that if I didn't at least gain some semblance of control, I would be blowing my load before I'd even gotten her off.

And that just wouldn't be fair.

Not when she'd gotten me off so nicely in my living room just a short time ago.

I pulled out, even though I think I died a little inside when I did so and moved down her body.

I nibbled on her belly, pulling lightly on the soft curves there, and then moved down the moment she giggled.

Her hands went to my hair, and right then, I contemplated never cutting it again.

When I'd gotten home from this last 'deployment', I'd let it go a little wild. But I really didn't like it *this* wild…not until she buried her fingers deep into my hair and cried out with a wild passion that was making my heart race.

"Ahhh, God," I growled. "You smell so good."

"That's the lube," she giggled again.

"No," I disagreed. "I know exactly what that smells like, and though I do smell it, I smell you more. You," I dropped my mouth down to hover just above her clit. "Smell like sugar cookies. Why is that?"

"I have this female, errrr, lotion," she explained. "I bought it online with my vibrator. It's supposed to cleanse as well as help it remain 'fresh.'"

Well, it smelled fresh.

It also smelled fucking edible.

"Goddammit," I growled. "I don't know what I was ever thinking. This pull you have toward me," I dropped a kiss directly on top of her clit. "It's something out of this fucking world. I never stood a freakin' chance."

Her hands tightened in my hair, and I started to swirl my tongue around her sensitive clit. Round and round, one, two, three. Four. On the fifth I stopped and sucked it into my mouth, flicking it with my tongue as I did.

Her thighs slapped up around my ears, trapping me in.

Little did she know that I never wanted to leave.

I'd gladly stay right here for the remainder of my life if I could manage it.

"I need you inside of me, please," she gasped through a breath.

I snaked one hand up and parted the lips of her sex, then used the other hand to breach her entrance with one single finger.

She went off like a bomb.

One second she was there, and the next thing she wasn't.

Janie had left the building, and it was a beautiful thing to watch.

After she rode out that orgasm on my hand, I pulled it out of her pussy and brought my fingers up to my lips, tasting her one more time as I settled back between her thighs.

My cock was kissing her entrance, but I didn't push back inside. Not yet.

I wanted her eyes when I did.

Which she gave me moments later as they blinked lazily open.

I bent down and pressed my lips against hers, a soft kiss, nothing more.

She started to tear up as I pulled away.

"What's this?" I asked her gruffly.

She swallowed and lifted her hips, causing my cock to pierce her sheath.

"It just doesn't seem like this is real. It's like I'm dreaming. Everything I ever wanted is right here. You're giving it to me…and I just feel like at any second it could be taken all away again." She lifted her hand and placed it against my racing heart.

I slowly filled her back up, this time just as easy as the first, and stopped once I was planted all the way inside.

"What we have is real," I promise. "I've done a lot of avoiding of you over the years, but don't ever think that I didn't want you. At first, when you were young, you were just a passing thought of 'she's sweet.' But when you matured? Yeah, those passing thoughts turned into a whole lot more. Now, you're not the only one disbelieving. Every time I've had you," I ground myself into her to remind her what it was we were doing, not to mention how good it felt. "It's like the first time all over again. You're like a piece of glass that all the adults told me not to touch. Yet, the moment I had you in my hands, I realized why they didn't want me to touch you. You're it for me, and I think they knew that. I think, in all honesty, that this was something they knew was going to be inevitable for us. At least on my end, that's why I stayed away. I didn't want to chance doing anything that'd get me killed."

Her laugh was husky, and the muscles deep inside of her tightened around my cock.

I closed my eyes as I tried to, once again, fight off what was inevitable.

And I didn't succeed.

"Fuck, fuck, fuck," I said repeatedly.

Instead of fighting it off, I let it come.

I started to fuck her in hard, fast strokes.

Her body jolted with each thrust, and I went up onto my hands as I watched her breasts bounce.

My eyes traveled down her body, taking everything in.

The way her pussy spread nice and tight over my cock. The way her clit protruded, still aching and throbbing. Her glistening sex, and her heavy breathing.

Her nipples were peaked, and her eyes were hooded.

Everything that I was feeling, she was feeling, too.

"Make yourself come," I ordered.

Her hand slid down her belly to come to a rest just above her pubic bone. Two fingers started to circle around her clit, and the entire time, she kept her gaze on me.

I picked up the pace. Watching, taking everything in, and waiting.

The moment I felt her tighten around me with her impending orgasm, I finally let go.

My release poured out of me in thick jets, filling her up and making her even wetter for the taking.

My abs bunched, and my eyes squeezed shut.

The breaths coming out of my throat were ragged, and I felt lightheaded.

"Fuck, baby," I breathed. "God."

I lowered myself down on top of her, loving it when her legs curled around my hips and tugged me closer.

Our skin was slick with sweat and other things, but neither of us cared as we came down from our high.

"I love you."

My words caused her to freeze.

"You...what?"

I grinned and tilted my face up, so she could see the sincerity in my eyes.

"I love you," I repeated. "I love you like a fat kid's pants like to dig into his gut."

She started to giggle.

She'd been doing that a lot.

Giggling.

I fucking loved it.

"Well?" I waited impatiently.

"Well what?" she asked.

"What about you?"

I knew she loved me. She knew she loved me. Hell, the entire town of Kilgore and Hostel knew we loved each other.

"I guess I love you, too." She paused. "You dirty old man."

I pinched her ass, causing her to shriek.

"Hey, not nice!" she said.

"When,"I dropped back down to whisper my words against her ear. "have I ever claimed to be a nice person?"

When I leaned back, I found her eyes were shuttered once again.

Shaking my head, I pulled away and took her with me until we were both leaning up on the bed.

The bed that was a huge mess, and sheets that would definitely need to be washed before we went to sleep in them.

"Tell me like you mean it," I ordered her, lightly tugging her hair.

"You're the window to my wall," she said with a growing smile.

I studied the ceiling.

"Yeah?" I asked in confusion.

"I'm the sweat that drips down your single ball."

I blinked.

"Skeet skeet."

I burst out laughing, then I reached for the pillow and smacked her with it.

She dramatically fell over clutching the pillow to her breasts.

"You weren't but a baby when that song came out," I grumbled as I stood up and headed to the bathroom.

"Hey!" she yelled as she followed me. "I was little, but that was a very impressionable time in my life."

I turned around, caught her by the hips, and walked with her into the shower that I just turned on.

She shrieked as the cold water met her back, but her nipples pebbled nicely.

"Shut up," I ordered. "You make me feel like a pervy old man every time you remind me how old you aren't."

I let her slip down my body until both feet rested on the tile of my bathroom floor.

"Well," she replied. "It could be worse."

"I'm not sure how your age could be any worse at this point," I admitted.

"I could be pregnant."

I stared as my heart started to pound.

"You're on birth control," I said to her, somewhat desperately.

She smacked me.

"I know that," she said. "But what I'm saying is I could be pregnant, and people could be thinking you got your daughter pregnant."

I placed my hand over her face and pushed her head back into the showerhead spray. "Just stop talking. I don't think my heart can live through your scenarios."

Janie was too busy laughing to reply.

CHAPTER 18

I think today is the day...that I burn this motherfucker to the ground.
-Text from Janie to Rafe

Janie

Tired, sore in the best of ways, and wide awake, I lay in bed next to Rafe listening to him breathe.

My dogs were snoring—on the floor at his side of the bed—and it seemed like I was the only one still not finding sleep.

I looked over at the phone on the nightstand. His. It stayed slightly illuminated, always displaying the time. I winced when I saw the time. 0333. Three freakin' thirty in the morning.

Ouch.

After waiting for the sheets to be washed, and then dried, we'd both fallen into bed with exhaustion.

Only, I didn't fell asleep like he did.

It was a good thing I worked from home because when I did finally get up in the morning I wouldn't be a very good functioning member of society.

But, as three thirty moved to four thirty, and all I had done was rethink the entire night through—I realized I might as well be practical.

Getting up carefully and quietly as possible, I made my way out of the bedroom and closed the door behind me. Once in the living room, I picked up Rafe's sweatpants from the laundry basket on the floor and slipped them on over my legs. I had to even untie the string because they wouldn't fit otherwise. They were very long, though, bunching up around my feet to about mid-calf.

Telling myself not to think about my curvy self—and when I say curvy I meant very curvy. It was more than obvious I enjoyed tacos a little too much—I took a seat on the couch and reached for my computer. Which was next to Rafe's computer.

I smiled when I saw the difference between the two. Where my computer was silver and covered in a hot pink skin with stickers over every available inch, Rafe's was boring and plain. The only embellishment on it whatsoever was the Apple symbol in the middle. And he didn't even put that there—Apple did.

Grinning to myself, I signed into my computer and immediately groaned. It was running slow again. Which irritated me.

I kept this bad boy in tip-top shape. It shouldn't be running slow.

Which got me curious. Why was it running slow?

An hour later I'd torn my computer apart—not literally, but cyberly—and was no closer to figuring out why.

The last thing I could try needed to be done through someone else's computer.

I looked over to see Rafe's just sitting there, and grinned.

Leaning over, I snatched his up and then spent twenty minutes hacking into it.

Who needed that many password protections?

Apparently, Rafe did.

But whatever.

And his password. My god. Who actually used that many special characters, uppercase and numerics? My man. He was *that* weirdo. If I had a password like his, I'd spend half my time trying to figure it out.

Sheesh!

However, once I was in, everything was pretty straightforward. Until I clicked on the app that was running and saw…myself.

I froze.

Then I looked over at my computer screen. And back over to his.

What the fuck?

"You're a little stalker, Rafe!" I whispered into the empty room.

I was honestly…proud.

Not mad, per se, but surprised. Surprised to find that he cared enough to track my computer—and me. It was honestly smart because my computer never left me. And this program he was running had to be the reason behind my computer running slow.

That little shit!

Shutting his computer down and acting like I hadn't touched it or realized a thing, I went to work on a few projects for Free. I'd been working for a little over an hour and a half when Rafe emerged, my dogs closely at his heels.

"You ever go to sleep?" he questioned, his voice husky and full of promise.

I smashed my lips together to keep from belting out my wishes and demands until I had myself under control, then said, "I tried. It didn't work out. So, I started working. And for some reason, I'm not the least bit tired yet. Though that could be the five-hour nap I had at five in the afternoon yesterday. I'll probably crash here in a few, though."

Rafe's lips twitched as he started walking toward the kitchen, which was directly behind me.

"Guess it's good that you don't have to go to work like I do," he mentioned.

"You don't actually have to go to work," I told him. "You're just going to work because you want to at this point."

He'd been working for the repossession company, Hail Auto Recovery, for a while now. Months and months longer than he actually had to.

At least I thought that was the case.

There was really no telling with how little he told me about his jobs.

"At this point, I work there because it's a good cover. Not to mention I get good insurance," he replied lazily.

I watched as he reached for his coffee mug—one of his favorites seeing as he had eighteen in the cabinets, yet always chose to wash that one—and pushed it underneath the Keurig's spout.

"You know," I told him. "It kind of surprises me that you have a Keurig. I would've figured you for a pot of coffee a day drinker, like my dad."

He gave me a raised eyebrow that clearly relayed his non-amusement with the statement and went back to his cup.

Once it was filled, he brought the cup up to his nose, inhaled the aroma, and groaned.

I swallowed, thinking about the last time he'd groaned like that—when he was inside of me—and felt things clench.

"When you look like that, I'm not sure how to respond," he said. "My initial response is to barrel toward you, spread your legs, and make myself at home. But trying to be a bit more laid back while recognizing the fact that your father will probably kill me if he sees a bruise on you has me, instead, staying over here and trying to think about things that'll make my cock deflate."

I snickered. "I don't want anything that has to do with my father to take first place in our sex life. If it feels natural to you, just do it."

He took a step forward, reaching his arm out to place his cup on the counter, and headed toward me.

I grinned, pushed my laptop to the side, and then made him late.

Forty-nine and a half minutes later, I was satiated. Well, and thoroughly.

"I gotta go," he said as he zipped up his pants. "Lying there, looking at me like that, isn't the way to make that happen."

I stretched lazily in the bed, rolled over on my belly, and then closed my eyes. "It's best that you're leaving. I'm tired."

His chuckle of amusement followed him around the room.

I felt the covers fall into place over my back, then Rafe whistled.

I turned only my head and saw Rafe calling my puppies to him.

He patted the bed, and both of my babies jumped into the bed with me, Glock on one side, and Kimber on the other.

"I named them after you."

He looked over at me.

"Yeah?"

He sounded confused.

I grinned.

"The first time I saw you, you were carrying a Glock. The second time I saw you, you had that Kimber. The one with the slide that has the oil slick-looking finish. I thought it was pretty."

His mouth opened, then closed, then he settled on a smile. "I kind of like that."

I closed my eyes again as Kimber's nose dug into my shoulder—just like she always did when we were at home in our bed—and I went boneless.

"Love you."

I blinked my eyes open again to see Rafe fully clothed now.

He was leaning over me, his mouth inches from my face.

I pursed my lips, and he grinned.

He didn't hesitate, placing his lips on mine, though.

"Love you, too." I stared at him for a long moment, my heart hurting. "Be careful. Don't do anything crazy."

He winked. "I'll try."

The remembrance of that day at the hospital, the worry I felt when I spoke with his doctor…it was still there. That feeling of impending doom.

I'd probably always worry about it.

It'd always be there, in the back of my mind.

But then he whispered, "I love you," one more time, and I forced myself to calm.

My eyes fell closed, and the next time I opened them, it was to find the room empty—long empty—and the dogs now growling somewhere in the living room.

I got up, slipped on a t-shirt of Rafe's from the night before, and snatched my phone which Rafe had so helpfully plugged in some time after I'd passed out.

With Rafe's name pulled up for a quick dial, I made my way out into the living room to find someone standing in it.

Found her standing in it.

She was in the process of taking her shoes off, and she had her purse in her hand as if she was about to drop it onto the coffee table.

"Can I help you?" I asked, pressing Rafe's name on the phone.

I was fairly sure that this wasn't going to get ugly, mainly because I could more than handle myself thanks to my father's and uncles' instruction, but I figured Rafe would want to know that someone had come into his house.

Also, that she'd done it seemingly without breaking in, because I would've definitely heard had that been the case.

I also knew for a fact that she didn't have a key—at least one that Rafe had given her—because Rafe had flat out said he hadn't given her one. Not before when he'd had his memory, and not after when Elspeth had played *While You Were Sleeping* on him.

Elspeth froze at my words and looked up, a look of horror on her face. "What are you doing in Rafe's house?"

I blinked. "Well, I actually came here legally. You, on the other hand, have not. Which, I might add, is *illegal*."

Elspeth blinked. Then a flush started to crawl up her chest—which was entirely exposed. Who the hell wore tank tops in the middle of December that looked like that?

Nobody.

It was dental floss at best.

The pieces of triangles that were covering her nipples were just enough to cover the areolas and not much more.

It was also white. Meaning that I could see those areolas.

They were dark. Like, almost black.

Was that normal?

Yes, Elspeth's hair was black, and mine was blonde. But her skin tone wasn't much different from mine.

Maybe even a little lighter, maybe.

I hated her.

"This is my fiancé's house."

I snorted. "Your fiancé my ass. You damn well know that you made that shit up," I said. "You do realize, right, that he was bound to remember sometime. Not to mention he's *mine*."

"I'm sorry, but he's not yours. He's mine."

"Negative," I disagreed. "He's mine. Has been for a very long time," I said.

Rafe and I had spoken about how he'd deal with Elspeth when the time came—though we had always planned on him actually being here when the discussion took place—and it was decided that whatever avenue he was trying to use with Elspeth was now at a dead end. He wouldn't be able to pretend to like her when he very much didn't, and I was okay with that. Anything that kept him away from this woman was okay with me.

"I beg to differ." Elspeth crossed her hands over her chest, making the barely-there fabric stretch even thinner.

I put the phone to my ear to ask a question, but Rafe's words caught my attention.

"That's so fucking hot," Rafe growled when I placed the phone back to my ear.

"What is?" I heard a man reply.

"She just claimed me."

I found myself smiling despite my anger at the situation. "She claimed you as her daddy?"

At that, I burst out laughing. "Who is that with you?"

Rafe snorted. "That would be Parker, the bundle of sunshine and flowers."

"Fuck you," I heard him say.

"She's not leaving," I finally said. "Is there something I should be doing? Calling the police?"

"I'm about two minutes at most away. I'll handle it when I get there." Rafe's words were abrupt and curt, letting me know that he wasn't happy that she'd just walked into his house.

"Okay," I said.

Then I dropped the phone to my side. "He's on his way. If you don't want this to get ugly, I'd suggest heading on out before he gets here."

"Oh, no thank you. I want to know why he'd do this to me," she sneered.

I rolled my eyes and leaned one hip against the couch. "Then, by all means, make yourself at home."

Elspeth did, but the moment her foot edged in the couch's direction, my dogs started their low, menacing growl again.

My lips twitched.

Then the door opened behind Elspeth moments later, and Rafe's large frame filled the door.

Oh, and he didn't look happy.

Not. At. All.

He glared at Elspeth. "I said everything I was willing to say to you at the hotel. You have absolutely no reason to be here."

Elspeth's lips parted to say something, but Rafe cut her off. "Get.

Out."

Elspeth uncrossed her hands and put them on her hips. "I don't think so. You owe me."

"I don't owe you a goddamn thing," he replied. "You owe me an apology, and you also owe Janie one."

Elspeth's lips twitched as if in amusement. "I saved your life."

"You didn't save a goddamn thing," he replied.

"Oh, well then, I guess I'll just take that order back then," Elspeth hissed.

"What order?"

That came from not Rafe, but from the even larger man behind him.

The man was huge.

I'd seen him before, of course.

His name was Parker. He'd said about eight words to me at most, and he made me supremely uncomfortable mostly because he was so intense.

Anything he said or did, I felt like I was being dissected and studied.

Like he was taking in everything and deeming me as unworthy.

Elspeth grabbed for her purse.

She walked out, and neither man said a word.

She got to her car, which was parked where Rafe usually parked his bike—in the fucking grass right up next to the house—and turned. "You'll regret this."

Rafe snorted. "Oh, I already do."

At Rafe's darkly murmured words, Elspeth got into the car.

But there was something in her eyes that made me feel like this was going to get really, really ugly.

Parker agreed with me.

I couldn't figure out whether that was a good thing or not.

CHAPTER 19

The day a man makes me happier than chips and queso is the day
I'll get married.
-Janie, Age 11

Rafe

"Uhhhh," Janie's hesitant voice said into my ear. "Could you do us a favor?"

I looked at my watch. I had exactly an hour and a half before I needed to meet my sister for lunch. "It depends on whether it'll take less than an hour."

"It should," came her instant reply. "It's pretty easy."

"Hit me," I said, my eyes scanning what was flowing over my computer screen.

I was looking over communications between Layton and one of his associates. They were talking in code, but eventually, I'd be able to break whatever it was they were discussing. Then I'd take them down.

"My dad needs a ride from the hospital. Shiloh and I are in sort of a situation," she said.

My heart started to race. "What kind of situation is it that it would keep both of you from picking your father up?"

"The kind where we're currently ankle deep in spa waters," she hesitated. "And my dad asked us to ask you. Apparently, you don't treat him like an invalid."

The doctors had decided to go ahead and remove James' gallbladder. It was discovered that he had hundreds of gallstones, and it was a miracle he hadn't had an attack before then.

"I guess I can. If he takes too long to get in my truck, I'll force him to go to lunch with me." I chuckled.

Janie snickered. "Your sister will be fine with that. She feels bad."

"How do you know that?" I questioned.

I knew she and Raven had been in close contact since we'd made this official—Janie and I. Raven wanted to make a good impression at first, and now I think it was that Raven genuinely cared about Janie.

Though, neither one had actually told me that they were talking to each other. I was just observant.

"Uhhh," Janie hesitated. "I gotta go. My dad needs to be picked up at one."

I shook my head in laughter. Janie was trying to mend bridges. Raven was trying to work through her inner demons. Though, she still blamed me for leaving her. And probably always would.

And, since I still felt bad about not being able to fight for her, I took her shit and hung on.

Because, despite my angry words when I found out Raven didn't tell me about Janie, I loved my sister. I loved her despite how she'd treated me for the last ten years.

Forty-five minutes later I was pulling into a spot that was as close as I could get to the hospital doors.

He wouldn't appreciate me pulling around, but I could finagle a closer parking spot without it looking like I was catering to his weakness.

Minutes later I walked into his hospital room and nearly laughed.

"Don't just stand there and watch me, fucker. Come and help me," James ordered.

I walked up to him and pulled his IV out. He'd already started it halfway, so I wasn't really doing anything that he hadn't already started.

Technically.

"You got a Band-Aid?" he asked.

I raised a brow at him and snorted. "Do you think I just carry Band-Aids around with me like dollar bills?"

He gestured with his head for me to go get one, and, rolling my eyes, I did.

I threw a handful at him and turned to survey his room.

"I'm early. But what the fuck? What's with all the flowers?" I asked. "I don't have enough room in my truck for all these."

James snorted. "I have the nurses picking them up and taking them to a few other patients that don't have the number of concerned visitors who think it's appropriate for a grown male to have so many goddamn flowers that I do."

I snorted.

"I swear to God. I tell them to stop sending flowers up here, and they send more. They think it's fuckin' funny."

"And who are these offenders?" I questioned, amusement lacing my voice.

"The fucking SWAT team, mainly the Spurlock brothers, Benny Bear, Nico, Luke and the god-awful Red-Headed Bastard."

My lips twitched. "Isn't that the entire SWAT team you just named off?"

He shrugged. "We're getting older. We have a few younger guys, but they're not at the others' level just yet."

"They gotta learn sometime. Y'all aren't always going to be able to do what you do," I told him. "Hell, even I can't do what I used to do. Twenty years ago, hikes with my gear over twenty miles was nothing. This last time I was there and had to do that, I thought I was going to die. Then there are all these little boys at my side, holding fucking conversations while I can barely fucking breathe. I gotta admit, it's a young man's game now."

James grunted in reply. "Don't fucking remind me. And don't think that I like that some old man is dating my daughter."

So, we were going to do this now? I guess I could get down with that.

"No warnings?" I waited for the inevitable 'hurt her and I'll kill you.'

James looked over at me, grinned widely, and then shook his head.

"I'm not going to give you a warning," he said, crossing his arms over his chest.

"You're not?"

I was kind of surprised by this. I would've expected more from the man who is the father of the daughter that I was about to cross that line with. Only, he didn't offer me anything of the sort, instead, he shrugged his shoulders.

"No," he repeated. "I'm not."

"Why?"

Why couldn't I figure out how to keep my fuckin' mouth shut?

But seriously, why the hell wasn't he warning me off? He had to know what I wanted from his daughter. He, as well as a lot of the other people in this organization, didn't really like me much.

I was lucky 'Uniball' was one of the only things they called me in front of others. It could be worse.

"Because I don't have to warn you. If you hurt Janie, she'll take care of you. I won't have to lift a finger."

I found my first smile since I'd walked through the hospital's doors.

She really could take care of herself. I didn't have any doubt in my mind that she could.

"I guess that's true."

"It is," he assured me. "I taught that girl everything she may need to know. She knows how to shoot. How to hunt. And," he paused, looking over at me. "How to call for help."

I didn't miss *that* threat.

He would be there if his daughter wanted him there, and there wasn't a damn thing in this world I could do about it.

"Well, I'll just go ahead and tell you what I have to say, then."

James sat on the side of the bed, crossed his arms over his chest, and waited.

"When I met her, I knew she was someone special."

James scowled.

"And over the years, as we came into contact, I stayed away, but that feeling never left," I continued.

James' scowl became fierce.

Now came the moment of truth.

"This job—my last one that I ever wanted to do—my coup de grace, if you will, I was never meant to survive," I said. "Whatever Layton is involved in, it's big. So big, in fact, that I've been working for years to get to this moment. Little jobs, here and there. And last month, with Dante's case, I think it was pure accident that I was able to stumble on a single one of Layton's toes. He thinks he's hidden well enough, but he's gotten sloppy. He thinks he's untouchable, and I want to prove that he isn't."

"You're not going to do this alone," he said. "My daughter loves you. Has loved you since the day she saw your broken self enter our compound."

My lips twitched. "I don't have that plan any longer. I'm backing off. I'm leaving this particular ball of snakes to someone else for them to handle."

James' face went slack with relief. "Maybe your problem is that you're trying to do it legal. Sometimes, legal isn't always the way to go."

"If it's not done legal, if the root system isn't dug up completely, then that leaves other people planted to continue with the work. And a new fucking tree takes root," I pointed out.

James shrugged. "Maybe. Maybe not. But what you need to realize is that sometimes, the bad guy wins. Sometimes, what you need is another bad guy to fight for you."

"And you have one of those bad guys?" I drawled.

James stood up and pulled his phone from the pocket of his jeans. "Let me text Jack to see where ol' Joker is today. When I get his number, I'll let you know."

Joker was also known as Lynn, who happened to be a jack of all trades, and a man of many faces—or names, for that matter.

While we were on that subject. "You do know, correct, that your daughter has surpassed the master, right?"

James frowned. "What do you mean?"

"Janie learned everything that she knows from Jack and Winter…but she's better than they'll ever be. She has everything y'all need, yet you all aren't utilizing her full potential. You set her to meaningless tasks involving paperwork, yet you don't even know that she could do a whole lot fucking more than what you're giving her," I said.

James blinked. "She's never said…"

"She's never said because she knows that y'all won't let her do it anyway." I paused. "Which is stupid. She's going to do what she

---

wants, and then act like she's coloring between the lines. But, I think it's time y'all let her use what you gave her the power to use. Plus, she can get it done in about half the time as Jack—who, from what I have observed, would rather be doing stuff in the shop more anyway."

James opened his mouth, then closed it. "Why wouldn't she say something?"

"Would it have helped?" I asked. "Because from where I'm standing, watching through y'all's windows, there's no way in hell you'd let your own daughter get mixed up in what you work on— at least if you thought she wasn't as good as she is. But honestly, James…she's good."

"Then why'd you kick her off of your stuff?"

I grinned. "Because I don't want to lose her. I'm guilty of treating her exactly like you do…which is part of our problem, now isn't it?"

James sighed. "I'll try to figure out a way to let go of those strings a little."

The nurse came in moments later, and we were out the door moments after that, James riding in a wheelchair since it was 'company policy.'

I tried not to laugh the entire way.

The drive to his place wasn't bad. After the specifics of me dating his daughter were over, they turned to the case that I was working on with Trace, and what we were doing to uncover Layton's criminal workings.

I told him everything, not leaving a single thing out, and when I was done, I realized a few things.

I should've done this earlier.

Trace hadn't been enough, and we both knew it. But since I had nobody I could trust to work this case—that I was willing to put in jeopardy with me—I hadn't reached out for help. Having someone else know what was going on was quite comforting.

At least from a security standpoint.

Janie knew. Trace knew. And now James knew.

If something happened…

"What. The. Fuck."

I looked up to focus on the man that was waiting in the driveway.

Tegan.

I narrowed my eyes.

"Remember, he's a cop and we can't kill him," James said. "I might lose my job, and I like it. I get to retire in a few years."

My lips twitched.

"Now's probably a good time to go ahead and ask for…"

"You have my permission to marry my daughter." He paused. "But just sayin', you can pay for it. Right?"

I started to laugh. "Yeah."

"Good, because she did all that bullshit with him to get you to pay attention to her, and by doing that, she used a lot of my savings. It seems only fair that you pay for it since she did it because of you."

I could get down with that. "I have more money than God."

He looked over at me. "You're a prick."

Then I stopped my truck and got out, waiting beside it while James made his way around to the front.

"Can I help you?"

I left the door in between me and Tegan. Maybe with it there, I would be able to control myself. A barrier for stupidity, so to speak.

"Your dogs have gotten disturbing the peace complaints," Tegan said, gesturing to Glock and Kimber who were sitting quietly at the gate, looking for all they were worth like well-behaved pups that they weren't. "I was in the neighborhood, so I chose to run the warning by."

Tegan held out a white piece of paper.

"And who might this complaint be from?" I asked as James took the paper. "There are no 'neighbors' out here to complain."

Tegan bared his teeth at me. "It was a runner passing by. She felt that her life was in danger of the dogs jumping over."

"The dogs won't jump over a razor wire fence," I told him bluntly. "You can start handing out bogus complaints all you want, but it's not going to bring Janie back to you. You were just a filler for me…FYI."

Tegan's jaw tightened. "That's not what she said."

I snorted.

"I'm sure she wouldn't tell you that you were filler," I pointed out.

"Janie told me everything," Tegan countered. "Everything."

My brows rose.

"She told me that your father was a piece of shit, and ruined multiple families' lives with his Ponzi schemes. How you were on a vendetta to right the wrongs of your father. How you were misunderstood, and that you were trying to become someone that your father would never be. She also told me that you were her childhood crush…but I just didn't know that that childhood crush was an adult crush, too." He laughed. "I guess I should have, though."

I wasn't sure how Tegan had found this information out—though it wasn't hard if you asked the right people—but I knew Janie would never tell him anything.

I confirmed that moments later when James started to laugh. "I told you that, numbnuts. You didn't even know Janie had dogs."

The dogs wagged their tails.

"Don't come around here handing me bullshit." He handed the warning back, but Tegan refused to take it. "I know you're hurt. I know that you feel slighted. But let me tell you something, don't mess with my girl or my family."

Tegan turned to go. "Rafe isn't family yet, though, is he?"

I think that Tegan was expecting a different answer than the one James gave him. Hell, we both were.

"Rafe's been family for a while now." James paused. "You just didn't know it. Like everything else you were kept in the dark about."

Tegan got to his car and turned his eyes to me. "Don't think that I forgot that you assaulted a police officer the other day in that hotel."

I grinned. "I'm unsure of what you're speaking of, officer."

I wasn't stupid.

I knew that the dash cam was running—as well as the body cam that Kilgore required all of their officers to wear when they were on duty—and I knew that admitting that I hit him wasn't something that I should be doing on camera.

But I couldn't help but mention a few things to him that *he* did.

"Do you remember calling Janie a slut?" I asked.

Tegan paused getting into his car.

"What about calling her trash?" I asked.

"I was drunk. I can't remember what I said," he lied.

"Then if what you're saying is true, then maybe you can't remember what happened, exactly, either." I paused. "From my recollection, you fell and hit your face on your own knee."

"The camera at the hotel…"

"Isn't on the particular floor we were on due to it having four rooms on it. All of which are honeymoon suites," I pointed out. "Everything in that particular portion of the hotel is very circumspect due to the high probability of honeymooners getting a little frisky in the hallway. And honeymooners paying out the ass to keep themselves safe."

Tegan got into his car and drove away.

Moments later, I turned to find James staring at me.

"There are cameras in that hotel hallway."

I snorted. "I know. Or there were, anyway."

James shook his head, then went to the gate and typed in the code.

Moments later the gate opened, and he got back into the truck.

I did, too.

"I feel like I'm the winner here," James said, breaking the silence. "Maybe I'll pay for the wedding after all."

I snorted out a laugh.

"You can try," I taunted.

CHAPTER 20

Ending work-related emails with 'fucking dickbags' is apparently
unacceptable.
-Rafe to Parker

Rafe

"Are you sure you're okay with going?"

I looked at Janie over my shoulder. "Yes. What the hell is the big deal?"

"They're a little…much. Alpha as hell."

Janie and I were on our way to a Dixie Warden MC party. It was being held in Benton, Louisiana about an hour and fifteen minutes away, and all of the family—Free family anyway—was riding over there in a group.

"I've been penetrating organizations for a very long time, honey," I told Janie. "I've been working with Hail Auto Recovery for a while now. I've worked for the FBI, CIA, and a few other organizations as a contract agent. All of which had me dealing with a large group of 'alpha male men' as you call them. Trust me when I say I can handle myself."

Janie sighed, then closed her eyes.

"I'm tired."

"Then sleep," I told her, reaching for her hand.

She clutched onto it, then leaned over onto my arm, which was resting on my truck's console.

We'd originally planned on taking my bike, but James and Shiloh had ridden James' motorcycle, originally planning on leaving Scout and Rebel at home. But Tegan had ramped up his annoyance factor and had started sending cops out to the compound on bogus noise complaints.

And since everyone in the compound was coming to this 'family picnic' as Janie kept calling it, they didn't want to leave the two teens at home by themselves.

So, they'd hitched a ride along with us.

Which worked for me because it looked like it was about to rain anyway, and Janie didn't look like she was feeling too well.

"Is your head still bothering you?" I asked.

"Yes," she answered. "It's been bothering me since I stopped drinking coffee."

"Why did you stop drinking coffee?" I asked.

"Because it made my stomach upset," she said.

"Did you switch to a different brand or something?" I questioned.

"No." She shook her head. "I think it's all this stress with you. I think I have an ulcer."

"Ulcers are…"

"Okay. I used to get them a lot when I was a young kid. I'm prone to them," she said. "Sorry for you. So, don't stress me out."

I laughed. "Yes, ma'am."

"Maybe you should go to sleep so the rest of us can, too," Rebel murmured sleepily from her position in the back seat.

Janie flipped her off, but she didn't say anything else until we were pulling into the driveway an hour later.

The next twenty minutes went like this…

"Hi, how are you. This is Rafe. He's my man."

"Hi, Rafe. I'm ***insert woman's name here***. I'm so and so's wife."

"Hi, nice to meet you," I'd reply.

And, so, it went, until I'd met about eight million and two people out in the front driveway and yard.

The men, however, were a little different.

All of them, and I do mean all of them, wanted to know who the hell I was. Torren, the man who owned the house we were currently parked in front of, had narrowed his eyes at me and asked my 'intentions.'

At this point Janie had wandered away, giving me 'man time.'

Apparently, that 'man time' consisted of me getting the third degree.

By not one. Not four. Not even ten. By at least twenty men—some of those men including the boy-men that belonged to the men.

Janie was a very loved person, and all of them wanted to make sure that I had what it took to withstand them.

And, by the time I was finished and walking away to get a beer, I wasn't sure if I'd won them over or not.

Most likely not seeing as I was 'way too old' according to Silas.

Silas, who himself was 'way too old' for his wife.

But whatever.

I wasn't one to judge.

But, as I found the beer, and then meandered through the throng of women, children, and random dogs, I found myself steering clear of all the men. Which was how I found my way into a room where I could hear a piano playing.

I found the room and came to a halt in the doorway as I took it all in.

There was a large, open room with one single thing in it: a baby grand piano.

It looked like it cost a whack, too.

I'd never had anything as nice as that.

My father refused to buy me anything that I could possibly ruin. Not that I ruined anything. I feared for my life too much to ever do anything that could possibly draw his wrath.

So, I stayed silent, did what I was told, and played piano on the stupid piece of crap he'd found for me.

Then he'd put it into the garage, so he didn't have to hear my 'racket.'

I found myself wistful as I watched the girl play through her music, wincing every so often when she missed a note.

I stepped into the room and walked to the side, so I wouldn't walk up directly behind her and scare her. This way she would see me coming, and maybe not freak out.

The girl looked up, grimaced, but kept playing.

She was about eight or so, and clearly unhappy to be playing.

She was tapping at the keys, face looking hard, as she tried to play the music on the sheet.

"This blows," she said, slamming her hand down on the notes, making me grimace.

"Having problems?"

The little girl looked up at me, and I realized instantly who she belonged to based solely on how much she looked like the woman I'd just met—the one who'd opened the door. Tru.

"I suck," she said. "This sucks. I hate this sucky piano. But I'm being forced to finish because I refused to do it earlier. And now this is my punishment."

"Why?" I questioned, leaning a hip against the side of the piano.

My eyes trailed over the girl's stubborn features.

"Because my mother is forcing me to play, and it sucks," she said. "It's too hard."

"Is anything easy worth it?" I asked cautiously.

"Taking naps is easy," she said. "And those are always worth it."

She had me there.

My lips twitched.

"Scoot over."

She frowned. "I don't know you."

I shrugged. "I don't think I'd be in your house right now if I wasn't a person that was supposed to be here."

I mean, I had to pass by at least twenty fucking bikers to get in here…

She nodded. "Mommy wouldn't have let you in."

I agreed with a nod. That had been true, too. I'd been documented by no less than thirty women, too. Including this one's mother.

"Fine, I'm Ashe," she said, scooting over. "Do you know how to play?"

I tilted my head up and down once. "I do."

"Then show me what you got, because I'm this," she held up two fingers about a quarter inch apart. "Close to quitting. I might as well play soccer if it's going to suck this bad."

I would've held in the laugh if I could have.

But I couldn't.

It just burst free before I could try to choke it back.

"I'm glad someone finds my life amusing," she grumbled.

Apparently, the life of an eight-year-old forced to play the piano was not an easy one.

"I know you can't hold your hands quite like I do yet, but when you get older, and with more practice, you'll find that you can," I said.

Then I proceeded to teach her the basics. Something in which she'd likely already learned if she was taking lessons as she said. But, you had to have a solid foundation to be able to build on it.

So that was where I started.

"Wow," the girl breathed. "Can you play faster?"

I grinned. "Can I play faster?"

I then proceeded to play "Great Balls of Fire" by Jerry Lee Lewis and thoroughly impressed my student.

As well as the audience at my back that showed a few notes into the song.

***

Janie

My eyes followed Rafe's progress around the room, and toward the sound of the piano playing, and I grinned.

"I know that look."

I looked up to find Tru staring at me.

"What look?" I teased.

"The one where you look like your heart is walking around this room, and you want to go find it," she said. "You look like you're in love, honey."

"I am," I admitted. "But…I've always been in love. With him. At least for the last couple years since I could understand what love really was."

"So, this is him."

I looked over at Sebastian's wife, Baylee, and grinned. "This is him."

"He really is a lot older," she surmised. "But he's cute. And that graying thing he has going on is hot…just like mine. I swear to God; the first time Sebastian saw that gray in his beard he freaked. Your man looks like he rocks it, though."

Rafe really did.

Though most of his hair was still jet black, a few bright and shiny strands at his temple and top of his head were coming out. His beard, though? Yeah, that thing was rocking the gray beard hairs like crazy.

It was hot as hell, I had to admit.

And there was something to be said for an older man seeing as Rafe knew exactly what to do…

"Older men are better, in my opinion," Sawyer, my grandfather's wife, said with a smile, echoing my thoughts. "They know how to do stuff more…efficiently."

"Grosssssss," my stepmother, Shiloh, cried. "I do not want to hear how efficient my father is!"

Everyone burst out laughing, as they always did when this came up.

"I agree," Sebastian came up to Baylee's back and wrapped his arms around her shoulders, pinning her to his body. "Where's this Rafe character? I feel like he's been gone too long. We didn't scare him off, did we?"

I pointed in the direction I'd seen him go and then saw Sebastian's eyes narrow.

"What's he doing back there?"

"Bathroom?" I suggested teasingly.

"Hmm," Sebastian grunted. "Guess we'll have to check on him to make sure he didn't fall in."

Then he started to walk away while calling out for Torren in the next moment.

I sighed and started to follow, shaking my head at the two of them as they moved.

"Sometimes I wonder if y'all are actually grown men," I called to their backs.

Torren threw a grin over his shoulder at me.

Then all words were halted when we arrived in the hallway to hear a little girl's laughter, followed by Rafe's deep worded reply to that laughter.

"What the fuck?"

Torren sped up and came to an abrupt halt at what he saw in the room.

Sebastian stopped shoulder to shoulder with him, and I had to squeeze through shoulders and arms to see, too.

And what I saw was quite honestly amazing.

Rafe was showing the little girl a few things with the piano. A note. I wasn't sure because I had no clue what all that gibberish was about.

"Wow," the girl breathed. "Can you play faster?"

Rafe grinned at the young girl. "Can I play faster?"

He put his fingers on the piano, and then he started to play.

The first notes of the song started, and I found myself smiling wide.

Sebastian threw his arm around my shoulder and pulled me into his big, warm body.

I laid my head against his chest and watched as my man taught a little girl how to play *Great Balls of Fire* on the piano. You know, if she could actually see it. His fingers were moving so fast that I wasn't sure she was really even watching.

More like admiring.

Hell, we all were admiring.

"Where in the hell did that come from?" Torren, Ashe's father, said as he watched his daughter admire the way Rafe was playing. "I need him to teach her every week. I think this is the first time I've ever seen her sit there without fidgeting in some way."

"Or complaining," Tru muttered from behind me. "God that girl. She was the one who wanted to play, too. It's not like we forced her. We bought the piano…then she decided she'd rather do guitar instead."

I shook my head.

"You can't have him. We have him," came my father's reply.

I rolled my eyes again.

Were they seriously fighting over a man?

"I only need him once a week for about an hour and a half. That's it."

"You haven't seen his computer skills, then." Uncle Sam's reply came from the back of the room. "Or the way he can find out information like Silas once did."

Jesus, the entire hallway was filled with people!

"Like Silas still does, you mean," Torren countered.

I rolled my eyes.

"Fifteen years of piano lessons," Rafe said as he stood up and turned. "I sometimes play when I want to get rid of some of my frustration."

I blinked.

"You never told me you could play the piano!"

I grinned at my sister Rebel's outburst.

"He didn't tell anyone, apparently," I drawled.

Rafe rolled his eyes.

"Whatever."

"Play something else," I ordered.

"You'll have to get a few beers in me, first," he said. "Playing makes me think about old times, and old times aren't always good times."

I knew what he meant exactly.

And immediately grimaced at remembering just some of what he'd explained during the course of our relationship.

CHAPTER 21

I'm not always right, but you're more not right. Like WAY more.
-Janie to Rafe

Rafe

"How are the dogs?" A man called out, changing the subject.

The man with the multicolor eyes.

He'd obviously read the tension in my shoulders and was offering a change of subject so this wouldn't get any worse than it already was.

"They're great, Trance." Janie smiled. "Rafe's been really awesome about helping train them. Not to mention it's awesome since I don't have to send them away for that to happen."

Trance's brows went up. "You train dogs?"

I nodded. "Yeah." Then paused. "When I first started out as an independent contractor, I went in as a dog trainer. 'Helping' other military members learn how to work with their K-9 partners. To do that, I had to have a base knowledge of training, handling, things like that. I went through about six months of training with a certified trainer, and then went in and started with the military while simultaneously looking for a member of that team that was stealing the dogs and giving them to our enemies."

Trance's jaw tightened. "Please tell me you caught them."

I nodded. "Sure did. Found out that he'd stolen four dogs like that, then handed them right on over."

"And what happened to the dogs?" Janie asked.

I grinned at her and her soft heart.

"Three of the dogs wouldn't perform for them since they didn't know the commands. Those dogs were never recovered. Best guess, they killed them when they wouldn't. But we have no solid evidence to say that they made it. However, one did survive, but only because she was being beaten and forced to perform. They'd learned by the fourth dog. They were able to get the dog back, but she wasn't the same...they did, however, let the old handler take her home."

"Who was the old handler?" Janie asked, excitement in her voice.

"You know him. Parker."

The room went wired at the mention of that name, and it was all centered on the man that hadn't said much to me since we'd arrived.

His name was Loki. I'd gotten that much out of him.

But not much more.

"Is she okay now? Does she function well with the handler?" Trance asked, ignoring the obvious tension in his friend and fellow club member.

Trance's curiosity about the dog was too much and overrode his friend's obvious annoyance about something that I was missing.

"The dog is definitely different. More volatile. She doesn't work well with other dogs, so any time that she goes out, he has to put a muzzle on her. Women are a no go for her, too. The main abuser must've been a woman because Carmen freaks out if a woman is anywhere near her. So, vet visits are not fun for her, but overall, she's doing well. Watchful, always broody, but she loves Parker. Parker just won't ever be able to date or bring a female home without Carmen going all Cujo on her."

"That would suck," Johnny, Sebastian's son, said. "Never getting any in your own bed."

Baylee, Johnny's mother, slapped him upside the back of the head. "Go away."

Johnny laughed as he walked away, causing the rest of the group to join in.

Everyone, that was, but Dark and Broody with the throat slash.

But, without straight up asking him what his problem was, I wouldn't be finding out anytime soon what the fuck his issue was.

Luckily, once the subject changed, throat slash chilled.

He even participated somewhat in our conversation.

We ate. We drank.

And overall, I had a really good time.

Until about four hours into the night and the discussion of which branch of the military we were all in started up. And what we'd originally wanted to be.

"I always wanted to be a doctor in the Army," I admitted to the room as a whole. "When I was a young kid, that was always my go-to-answer. Then I grew up and found out that I loved computers. From there, I added it to my newly discovered list of skills and kept right on truckin'."

Torren grunted.

"I have a cousin in the Army right now. He's a doctor. Layton's always said that he doesn't like it," Torren murmured. "Something about having to work on soldiers that don't take care of themselves. Then again, Layton's a complete douchebag, so there's really no telling if what he says should be taken as true or just his bullshit spilling out."

"Layton Trammel?" Janie asked, a frown forming on her face.

My heart skipped a beat at hearing that name.

"Actually, yes. That's my cousin," Torren said. "Why?"

Janie's eyes met mine.

"Because that's the man that cost ol' Uniball his errr…ball," Sam offered.

Janie hissed at her uncle. "Stop calling him that, or I'll kick your ass."

Sam held up his hands in surrender. "Down girl. I was just sayin'."

"Well just say it nicer next time," Janie ordered.

I wrapped my arm around Janie's waist and pulled her down into my lap.

"What did I tell you?" I whispered into her ear. "It's okay."

She turned to me. "It's not."

"It is," I confirmed.

"Well, I guess we'll just have to agree to disagree."

We spent the rest of the night like that, blissfully unaware that our lives would change in just twelve short hours.

Lani Lynn Vale

CHAPTER 22

*You can tell a lot about a person whether they bring their mouth to
the banana, or the banana to their mouth.*
-Janie to Kayla

Janie

My eyes took in the road outside Rafe's house. There were cars
lining the entire road on each side. The house catty corner to his
had a shit ton of people milling about, and the mailbox had about
thirty balloons—pink ones. Pink ones that said, 'It's a girl!'

Smiling at Rafe's neighbors' pure happiness about having a little
girl, I walked up the front steps of his porch.

While I did, I wondered if Rafe would want to stay in Hostel.

It was just far enough away from my family that they couldn't pop
in, and close enough that I could drive back home in case of
emergency.

I could totally see myself living in a place like this. Wholly and
completely. It was small, but not too small. It had a taco shop, a
bank, a school, and even an ice cream shop. What else could a girl
like me want?

Not to mention the place Rafe had for himself was adorably cute. It wasn't anything like what I would've expected from him.

For some reason, I envisioned a minimalistic house with little fanfare. Something with clean lines, nice grass, but not much else.

The house he had for himself was the exact opposite. It was a three-bedroom farmhouse style. It was painted white with red shutters. Even the windows had planter boxes with actual real live flowers in it. Real live flowers that Rafe got up every single morning and watered shirtless while he drank a cup of coffee.

While he did this, the neighborhood ladies watched. Seriously, there were no less than six women from four different houses on Rafe's block that were always out on their porch. It was completely by coincidence, of course.

Kind of like why I always made sure to watch him from his bedroom window.

A bedroom window that had blinds *and* curtains.

Seriously, the man had his shit together.

He even had complete sets of cutleries in the kitchen. Nice furniture. There were even decorative hand towels in the bathroom.

And none of it was due to his sister coming in and fixing his house up. It was all his decorating skills. Though, his explanation was that he wanted people to think that he was planning to be there for a while. As a cover, he had to make it look "good."

I agreed, but he hadn't had to go to that level of "lived in."

But I liked it.

The porch would look good on a Christmas card. Me and him. A baby or two.

I smiled as I inserted my key and pushed open the door.

My first indication that things weren't right were my dogs' reactions.

They yipped and started to growl, causing me to look back at them with a frown.

I walked in and froze when I saw the clothes on the floor.

Not Rafe's. And certainly not mine. That bra on the floor wouldn't have even fit me in my teenage years when I was a normal boob size.

It certainly wouldn't fit me now.

Those panties that were next to the bra wouldn't fit either.

I stepped inside and saw the jeans and skimpy top next. And I knew exactly who they belonged to.

I walked over the clothes and followed my senses to Rafe's room.

And saw red.

Elspeth lay seemingly sated on the bed, and I could hear the shower running in the bathroom.

I walked calmly to the bed, then snatched Elspeth up by the hair.

Now, normally I wasn't a violent person. Really, I wasn't.

But something switched inside me. Some dark, hidden compulsion washed over me, and suddenly my rage was all consuming.

I was just so. Fucking. Mad.

Which was why I went all Hulk on her and lifted her fabricated sleeping ass right out of my man's bed.

"You manipulating whore," I said. "What the hell is it going to take to get it through your head?"

Elspeth "woke up" with a surprised shriek.

"Owwww!" she screamed. "Let go!"

Yeah freakin' right. I wasn't letting her go until she was out of the house.

And, as I led her through the house to the front door, I said, "You better grab your clothes as you pass them. Because otherwise, you'll be giving the neighbors a free show. Not to mention they're having a party across the street. You'll stick out like a sore thumb."

I didn't slow down even a little as I dragged her out with me toward the door.

And, surprisingly, she even managed to grab her jeans, purse, and bra.

Highly impressed, I opened the door, then gave a satisfying tug on her hair.

She went flying onto the porch, and I glared at her when she picked herself up. She turned around and started to come at me.

She froze, but that might also be because I got my concealed carry out to point at her.

"I'm literally to the point right now where I'll shoot you and deal with the repercussions later," I said. "I'm fairly positive I could thrive in prison."

I heard a snort from behind me but didn't give Elspeth the chance to do anything by turning around. Instead, I kept my serious eyes on her.

"Go."

Elspeth stood up, and that's when the neighbors across the street started to squeal. Not because of Elspeth's naked ass, but because of something else—a dog maybe.

I didn't pull my eyes away from Elspeth as she started to rush down the stairs.

In fact, I waited until she was in her car completely before I backed out of the doorway, closed the door, and turned my glare on the man behind me.

He didn't look pleased.

In fact, I would go as far as to say he was pissed.

But not at me.

At her.

Which only got me angrier.

I wasn't mad that I'd found that witch in his bed while he was in the shower. I knew they hadn't done anything. I also knew that he never would. Rafe just wasn't that type of man.

I was mad that he'd let someone into his house while he was vulnerable. He had no clue she was there, and *that* made me angry.

"What were you thinking?" I bellowed.

Rafe's brows went up.

"Nothing happened," he said. "I didn't even know she was here!"

"I know that, moron," I snarled. "You could've gotten killed! Don't you know how to lock your doors? Because I'm pretty sure if you did, you wouldn't have riff-raff coming in without your knowledge!"

He tilted his head. "I wasn't going to be killed."

"You were in the shower with literally nothing to protect yourself! You even left your gun on the bed!"

"Let me get this straight. You're mad at me not because I have a woman in my bed. Naked. But because she could've killed me while I wasn't paying attention."

I nodded, throat thick with my anger and a whole lot of worry.

"If you're going to do this to me all the fucking time, then I might as well leave now. It's like you don't even care about your life at all."

Rafe's eyes narrowed. "I'm a grown ass adult, Janie. In fact, I'm even more of an adult than you are. I'm forty-one years old. Swear to Christ, you don't even pay attention to that fact."

I wanted to scream at him for his nonchalance.

It was as if he didn't care that a good fright could kill him. As if he didn't have his days already numbered. I mean, he could possibly die at any moment thanks to a brain aneurysm—and he just didn't care.

It literally made me sick to my stomach to think about.

"I'm a grown man," Rafe repeated. "A grown ass man that has been taking care of himself for far longer than anyone can imagine. She was a slip of a girl. She was also naked and vulnerable. There is no way in hell she could overpower me. None."

I chose not to point out that at this point he was repeating himself. That probably wouldn't go over well.

"Well, I don't agree. That could've just as easily been a robber with ill will toward you. Someone with a gun. Someone that didn't want your dick, but your fucking wallet."

"Well, then I'll die."

It was the words "I'll die" that did it. I couldn't take it anymore. I just couldn't.

Getting my bag off the floor where I dropped it in my haste to get Elspeth out of Rafe's house, I picked it up then shouldered it. "Fine."

"Fine what?" he asked, anger lining his features.

"Fine. I'll fucking grow up. At my own house. For a few goddamned years."

With the way I was going, it'd be at least a year before I got over my anger. I was a grudge holder. I couldn't help it.

He just shook his head. "And maybe get rid of some of that childishness while you're at it."

My mouth fell open.

Then I just shook my head and turned to leave. Whistling as I did.

The final betrayal was Kimber refusing to leave Rafe's side.

I would've left her, too. But then Rafe had to go and show his superiority by telling her to go with me. Which she did.

And, as we drove away, she sat in the back seat and refused to look at me.

That was the final straw. I pulled over and cried.

***

Rafe

I found her on the side of the road crying. She'd made it literally four houses down before she'd pulled over.

I felt like an asshole for saying what I had. But goddamn. I was so tired of everyone acting like they knew what was best for me.

They didn't.

I did.

But Janie at least had my best interests at heart. That was more than I could say for the rest of my so-called friends and family.

I started walking to her car instead of taking the bike like I'd intended to do and arrived at her door within about a minute.

I looked at her through the glass and immediately felt like shit.

She was crying her eyes out, and she wasn't a pretty crier.

Which endeared her to me even more.

I tapped on the window, and she looked up.

She looked like I'd broken her heart.

I opened her car door, and she fell into me before I could even bend down.

She hadn't even taken the seatbelt off first.

"I'm sorry!" she wailed. "I was just so scared."

I reached across her body and released the belt, then disentangled her from the webbing before gathering her into my arms.

She buried her face into my neck, and I felt her tears sliding down my chest.

"You're not wearing a shirt," she murmured.

"I didn't have a chance. I wanted to catch you before you got to your dad and he decided to off me," I teased her.

Janie started to giggle. "He'd never do that. I think he secretly likes you. Or, maybe, what you can do for them, that is."

I laughed.

"Yeah, I think you're right," I agreed. "Do you want to…"

Janie's phone rang, and she pulled away with a frown.

"Who is that?" I asked curiously.

She showed me the screen readout, and I winced.

"Don't answer it."

Janie threw the phone down on the seat next to her without answering it.

"Turn around and drive back to my place?" I asked hopefully.

She nodded, and I stepped back far enough so she could close her door.

Moments later she pulled slightly forward, turned around, and headed back my way.

I walked back a lot slower than she drove, but she waited for me on my porch steps.

With her phone ringing again.

"Just answer it," I told her.

She handed it to me. "You do it."

I sighed and answered the phone. "I'm taking care of it."

"You better, motherfucker."

Then James hung up.

I sighed and handed her the phone, then turned back around. "Let me check the mail really quick while I'm out here."

Janie nodded but didn't move from the porch steps.

I passed Glock and rubbed his head, smiling when he tried to lick my hand.

"Gross," I told him.

He let his mouth fall open.

I'd just pulled out the mail—bills and a reloading magazine— when Janie's voice sounded.

***

Janie

"We should talk about what just happened," I murmured, dashing my hands one more time across my cheeks.

Rafe's lips kicked up. "Yeah. No. I think we'll just chalk what just happened up to Elspeth being a bitch and call it a day."

My smile wobbled. "I kind of…"

Rafe's face changed. His eyes, which had previously been smiling and soft, turned hard and angry.

In one split second, he went from the man that I knew to a killer that I didn't.

We were standing in his driveway. My dogs were poised in between us—Glock closer to me, Kimber closer to him. Rafe was standing at the end of the driveway next to the mailbox.

The neighbors' guests still lined the street, but one black panel van must've not belonged to the neighbors because men poured out of it and started circling us. Three coming for me. Three going for Rafe.

I froze as terror started to slide over me.

These men, all of them, were huge, buff, and covered in black. Their beards were bushy and thick, and not well maintained at all. Where Rafe looked like a bad ass, these guys just looked plain fucking scary.

My eyes sliced to Rafe, taking in his reaction.

In his haste to get to me, Rafe had left his gun. He'd also left his shoes, shirt, and anything else that might've come in handy for this situation.

"She was sent to get you quietly," the man closest to Rafe, the one that looked to be the leader of these band of misfits, said. "You should've let her do her job."

Rafe didn't say anything, but he'd crept closer to me. Suddenly, he wasn't the length of the driveway away. He was only a foot away. Reaching distance.

A sound of gravel grating at my back made me flip around, but it was only Kimber, menacing and silent.

I turned back around and crowded close to Rafe's back. The moment nothing separated us? I lifted my shirt and pressed my stomach against Rafe's hand, which was behind his back. He'd been reaching for me to make sure I was close.

He hadn't really needed to bother. I was as close as I could get without actually hindering his movements. I was practically in his arms.

The moment his hand felt my revolver, he closed his fingers around it.

It only held five shots. I'd always joked with my dad—if I need more than five shots, I'm screwed anyway. There's no way I would be able to get that many people all by myself.

But Rafe? He could. And suddenly I wished I had a semi-automatic with fifteen rounds in it. If anybody could do it, he could.

There were six men, five shots, and only one of him. I looked down at my side when I felt something brush up against it, and saw Glock there, letting me know that he had me.

I swallowed past my pounding heart and turned my attention back to the men, and what they were saying.

"…Layton wants you to know you're not as smart as you think you are."

My heart sank.

How had he found out?

Rafe was so careful. That's why he hadn't gotten anywhere in the months that he'd been on this case. He hadn't wanted to tip his hand.

Rafe's hand clenched around the butt of my gun, and he pushed against my belly with the tip of one finger.

I bent down and stepped away, the gun sliding free.

I went to step back forward, but he stopped me by shaking his head.

I remained where I was as I prayed that this wouldn't turn out the way I thought it was going to.

That this was only a discussion. That we were going to walk back inside and figure out just what in the hell was going on.

But, by the tenseness of all the men, including my man, I knew this wasn't going to work out like that.

My phone vibrated in my pocket, and I looked surreptitiously at my watch to see who it was.

Daddy.

I pressed answer on my watch, then hoped that since the volume was so low—I accidentally answered my phone a lot. And, most of those times were inopportune. Like, when I was going to the bathroom, or in the middle of my doctors' appointments. Sometimes, while I was sitting on the couch watching porn—and that had only been one single time, and lucky for me, it was Kayla that had called. Not anybody else.

I could hear my dad calling my name,

"Don't touch her," Rafe snarled, his body going tight like a bowstring.

I looked to my left to see one of the men try to get closer to me, but Glock turned his big body to block him.

If they got through my baby, they wouldn't get through Rafe…right?

I was literally shaking, and all the while my nausea rose.

I wasn't cut out for this.

I wouldn't be able to hack this part of the job. My dad was right.

I never, not ever, thought I would be agreeing with my father on the fact that I couldn't do what a man did, but I was right then.

Where I was shaking, sweating, and nauseous—and obviously showing the fact that I was scared to death, Rafe was cool, calm and collected.

He was staring blankly at the men around him, and he was anything but scared.

He was pissed.

"Go get his computer," GIC—guy in charge—ordered.

The man that'd circled around to my back took a step back, and then turned on his heel and rushed up the steps. He burst right through the door and disappeared inside.

"As for you, my friend Rafe, Layton would like to have a few words with you…with both of you," GIC said.

Rafe didn't reply. Didn't move.

Hell, I wasn't even sure he was breathing.

The sound of boots on the wooden steps made me turn my head to look behind me again, and what I saw nearly made me laugh.

The guy that'd gone to retrieve Rafe's computer had retrieved a computer all right.

He hadn't grabbed Rafe's computer, though. He'd grabbed mine.

Dumbass.

There was nothing on my computer but a bunch of mumbo jumbo. I kept everything backed up in the Cloud. Literally, the only thing they would find was my freakin' Solitaire addiction.

Rafe's computer, I was sure, was likely similar to my own.

However, there had to be a reason that they'd wanted Rafe's, otherwise, they wouldn't have specifically mentioned it as if he had something that they wanted.

So, if it wasn't in their hands, I was happy.

"All right, Rafe. Make this easy. Let's go, and we don't kill your girl," GIC said. "You both just come with me, and we'll make it out of here with everyone breathing.

"You leave her here, and I'll go with you," Rafe countered.

GIC shook his head. "No. We can't do that. Boss said you were both to come, so you both come. You know how orders are."

Rafe's hand clenched on the gun.

"No," Rafe repeated.

"Boys," GIC sighed.

Everybody moved at once.

Guns were drawn, but none of the four that had raised their pistols got any further than unholstering them.

Why?

Because Rafe had put a bullet in their skulls in less time than it took me to draw my next breath.

Everyone was frozen.

Everyone, that was, but Rafe…and apparently the guy behind me.

The guy behind me put his arm around my throat, and I was pulled back against him.

He spun and aimed, but it was too late.

The man had me exactly where he wanted me.

I could hear the rise of voices as the neighbor's music changed to country music, and I wondered if anybody would've heard those gunshots over all the racket they were making.

Our luck, probably not.

My eyes widened when the man at Rafe's back moved, but my puppies were on him before he could so much as take a threatening step.

Kimber had him by the arm that was raising the weapon in the air, and Glock was at his throat moments later.

Then suddenly, it was just one.

"Get in the van," the man said. "Now."

Rafe swallowed, then started backing away.

"I'll get in the van if you let her go."

"Drop the gun," the guy ordered.

Rafe threw it underhanded across the yard, and it landed in the flower bed with a soft thud. Then he backed away until he was standing next to the van.

"Call the dogs," bad guy number six ordered. "I have some rope in the van. Tie them to the mailbox."

Rafe hesitated, and the guy with his arm across my throat cocked his gun.

Rafe reached into the van and got the rope.

Then he called the dogs to his side and tied them to the mailbox.

Rafe waited for his next order, which, apparently, was to get in the van.

"In the back. There's a set of handcuffs. Cuff both hands to the pole back there."

Rafe made eye contact with me.

"How do I know you won't hurt her?"

Bad guy grunted. "You don't."

Then he pressed the gun to my forehead harder.

That was about the time that I lost my battle with the nausea.

It hit me so fast and hard that I was projectile vomiting all over my captor, as well as all over Rafe's front walk.

My captor pushed me away with a shove and started walking away from me.

Moments later, the van with Rafe inside was gone.

And I was left standing alone with five dead bodies in Rafe's front yard, with vomit covering me and everything around me in a five-foot radius.

Before I could freak out, though, a police cruiser pulled up.

large, tanned man got out in police uniform, took everything in, and went for the mic on his shoulder.

"This is Unit-56. We're going to need additional units. The father was right."

My father!

"Daddy!" I said, reaching for my phone.

My father came onto the line in less than an instant.

"Janie, are you okay?"

"I-I'm okay. Rafe…Rafe went with him."

"I know, baby. We're already working on it," he said. "Is the detective there?"

"Detective?"

The phone was taken from my hand, and the large tanned man—who I now realized wasn't exactly tan, but more of a mocha color thanks to his heritage that had nothing to do with the sun. "This is Detective Tyler Cree."

I kept my eyes above and marched down to my dogs, and the moment that I was within reach of them, I dropped down to their level and hugged them.

Then, immediately burst out crying.

"Oh, God."

***

Two hours later

"I already told you. They came out of a black panel van. One of those new ones that look kind of cool. They surrounded us, then one of them went inside to get my computer."

"Why your computer?" Detective Cree asked.

I shook my head. "He didn't actually want my computer. He wanted Rafe's, but the guy found mine instead. I saw him pick it up from where he'd dropped it on the ground. It was mine. See? Rafe's computer is right there."

I pointed to his simple black laptop that'd been sitting on the end table.

Detective Cree nodded. "We'll have to take that into evidence with us. See if we can pull anything useful off of it."

A thought occurred to me, and I jumped up.

"Janie?" my father called.

I rushed to the laptop, flipped it open, and rushed back to the table. Setting it down where I'd been originally sitting, I started tapping away.

"Now, the other night, I was looking at my computer and I was annoyed with how slow it was running. Thinking it might've been something else, I picked up Rafe's computer and found this program. The program tapped into my computer and allowed it to see everything that I was doing. It even has a..."

"Camera," my father said, sounding pissed.

"Don't get all pissy, Daddy," I ordered. "And aren't you kind of glad he had it right about now?"

"Should let him fucking rot," he said stubbornly. "That's an invasion of privacy, Janie. No joke. You shouldn't be so nonchalant about this."

My brows rose, and I said, "You remember that time when I was sixteen, and I found out that you installed that tracker on my car, as well as on my phone and purse?"

My father tightened his lips with displeasure.

"Got you there, bad boy," Elliott replied. "Now, what do you need from us, Cree?"

Detective Cree narrowed his eyes at Elliott. "Who are you?"

Elliott's lips twitched. "Someone you'll want on your side. Trust me."

Detective Cree didn't look like he agreed, but then I stopped paying attention to whatever they were talking about and started pulling up the program on Rafe's laptop.

Moments later, I saw a man's face.

"That's him," I said, backing away slightly, startled to see him so close.

"Who's that?" Detective Cree asked.

"That's the man that took Rafe."

"And that one?" He pointed to the man standing behind the guy's right shoulder.

"That, I'm assuming, is Layton," my father replied.

I pulled my phone out to access my files that I'd gathered on Layton Trammel and then turned it to compare the two men.

"This one is his latest military photo," I said. "That one is him, correct?"

"This photo does match his hair—though it's gotten longer. The eyes are the same, too," Dad said.

"Then," I nodded in confirmation. "I think I'm fairly positive that the man standing at his shoulder is Layton Trammel."

I turned my eyes to Detective Cree, waiting for his response.

"We'll get some units to his house."

With that, he stood up and walked to the door, then exited it without another word.

I turned to my dad, as well as the rest of the men that came with him. Uncle Sam. Max. Jack. Elliott and Gabe.

All of them were there, and I couldn't help but be relieved that they were.

I knew that this wouldn't go badly if they were here.

This group of men standing there, looking down at me with angry looks in their eyes, never gave up.

Not until they got what they were searching for.

"He's not at his house," I said to them.

My dad tugged on my ponytail. "No, he's not. Go take a shower. Wash that blood and vomit off of you. When you're done, we'll start tracking where he's at. You can do that, right?"

I nodded and typed a few things into the computer, then referenced those data points onto my phone. "It says he's about an hour north of here in the middle of about a thousand-acre nature preserve."

I showed the phone to them, and my father took it.

"You didn't want Detective Cree to know this?"

I laughed. "When have we ever done things the way they were supposed to be done?"

With that, I allowed my father and my uncles the privacy they wanted and walked to the shower.

On the outside, I was cool as a cucumber. On the inside, I was about to vomit again.

Did vomit again.

Score another one for the bad guys.

CHAPTER 23

If I have to put on pants for you to come to my house, then you're clearly not that good of a friend.
-T-shirt

Rafe

"Goddamn ticking time bomb," Trace muttered over and over again. "Jesus Christ. Whatever you do, don't freak out, okay?"

I had absolutely no idea what he was babbling on about.

When I'd walked into the room on my own, the first thing I'd seen was Trace. He'd been sitting in a chair, much like I was, and his eyes were directed at the door. Waiting.

He had his hands tied behind his back which was then attached to the metal chair he was sitting in.

Much like I had now.

I tested the knot of the rope one more time and felt it tighten farther.

Fuck!

"Are you sure you're okay?"

I looked at my friend, and if my hands were free, I'd punch him square in the face.

I shook my head. "Trace, I literally have no fucking clue what you're carrying on about. I don't have a ticking time bomb in my head. I'm fine."

Trace shook his head. "The doctor…"

"It was the best thing I ever did," Layton drawled as he entered the room.

"What was?" I asked, spitting out a mouth full of blood next to his feet where he came to a stop directly in front of me.

"Telling your friends and family that you had an inoperable aneurysm was a great job on my part," Layton explained. "I told them that due to the recent head injury, that the aneurysm couldn't be treated because you were too unstable. I also made sure that they knew any upsets could also trigger it. They were to treat you with kid gloves, and not tell you a goddamn thing."

"You *what?*" Trace bellowed.

I looked at my friend and told him without words that he needed to chill the fuck out.

Trace's shoulders tightened, his eyes narrowed, but he shut his mouth.

"Why?" I asked, turning back to Layton.

"Because it left you vulnerable, and it alienated them from you," he answered. "Now you're all alone and nobody is here to save you."

It had.

I'd felt in the dark this entire time, and their refusal to tell me anything, even when I'd asked, had really brought back old feelings I'd rather have left buried.

Meaning just like the rest of them, Trace had known, too.

I clenched my jaw.

"It was your medical chart, you see." Layton's amused words made me want to punch him in the non-existent cunt.

The fucker.

"Elspeth begged me to look over your chart. 'Daddy, please look over him. I want the best taking care of the man I plan to marry.'" He mimicked his daughter's voice. "So, I did, for her. And you wanna know what I found?"

I closed my eyes as dawning understanding washed over me.

My sister was my point of emergency contact. The nurse on call had called her and asked for my medical history.

She'd likely given everything to her without a second thought.

Where I had been trying to keep myself under the radar, my sister had blown that cover sky high. Just by giving my medical history.

God. Fucking. Dammit.

Of all the chances.

Everything was starting to make sense.

The way that Janie lived life like she was going to lose me at any moment. The way she was capturing every single memory that she could.

Her request to have a baby.

Her promise that she would never, ever love another man.

Her desire to get married in Vegas.

Everything was all adding up, and I couldn't believe I hadn't put two and two together to get four until now.

"I see understanding is dawning." Layton grinned. "Fucking sucks, doesn't it, having all your hard work take a nose dive right in front of you."

He walked to the wall at my back, and I could no longer see him.

I could see Trace, though, who was tied just like I was, only facing me.

And Trace's face showed me that whatever Layton was doing back there, I wasn't going to like.

"I spent years setting this final payout up. Hundreds of thousands of dollars hidden. It was going to be the perfect retirement gift from the US Army. Even though they didn't exactly know that they were giving it to me. But still…this was going to be perfect. I had it all lined up. All my ducks in a row…then you happen along. Every single thing I had planned, you foiled. First it was the guns. Then it was the hack into my account. After that, it was the rerouting of not just my retirement, but all of my present wealth, too. And, on paper, it doesn't look like I lost a goddamn thing. That's where I was hoping your computer came in handy."

Layton came back around and stopped in front of me, a scalpel in his hand.

"You're going to use this computer and give it all back. If you give it back, I'll consider allowing you to live."

I hadn't done a damn thing with any of his money.

None.

I'd tried.

Oh, how I'd tried.

But I hadn't been able to get a fucking thing. It was all too random. There was no rhyme or reason to anything that Layton did.

I couldn't get a handle on a single thing.

I had a ton of information…and none of it made any fucking sense.

Yet, Layton apparently thought I knew something.

And maybe I did, and I just didn't know it.

I did know that I didn't have his money, though.

"You're going to use this computer, and you're going to get my money back to me. Now," he said. And, before I could so much as flinch, he sliced me from eye to chin. "Or I'm going to slice you up and make it hurt."

I felt the blood start to well on my face, and drip down my neck in a steady stream.

"I need my hands to do that," I told him honestly.

"One," he said, then walked around me while keeping the computer on the table, facing me.

The computer wasn't my computer. It was Janie's.

Thank God she didn't know about the program that I'd installed on here. Otherwise, I just knew she'd be watching what was about to happen next.

Because I wasn't going to find that money.

There was just no way around it. I couldn't. Not if I didn't know where it was.

And it wasn't like I could just give him that kind of money. I had a hundred thousand in the bank, sure, but not thousands and thousands.

My hand came free from the bindings behind my back, and I brought it forward.

A door slammed, and I lazily pulled my eyes up to see Elspeth standing there.

"Hey, y'all!"

Layton jolted.

I didn't. I'd seen her enter the room. Her eyes were taking in absolutely everything in one quick glance.

"What are you doing in here?" he barked, his eyes warily going to me and then Trace. "Who let you down here?"

"Oh, Daddy, Daddy, Daddy." Elspeth came swaggering into the room. "You don't think that I was going to allow you to get away with all this, did you?"

Layton looked stunned speechless.

"Your men aren't yours any longer. They're mine."

I blinked, unsure of what to do.

"What?" Layton said. "You're being ridiculous. Get out."

Elspeth smiled then. "I guess you could always try to kick me out."

Layton stalked toward her, and the man that had taken me stepped in front of her, blocking his way.

"No." He said a single word.

Layton didn't stop.

He kept coming.

And then his face was filled with a bullet from the man's gun.

"Bummer," Elspeth said as she watched her father fall. "I really had plans for him, you know. Seriously, Stav. I told you not to shoot him until I was finished."

"You're finished," Stav said.

Elspeth sighed.

Then she stepped over her father's rapidly cooling body and wrapped her arms around Stavros. "Give me a kiss. Then go let the feds know what's up."

Stav did what she said, and I watched it all with stunned disbelief.

The moment the man was out of the room, Elspeth turned those eyes to me.

"You'll have to thank your girlfriend for me. I really, really didn't want to do anything with you that might hurt mine and Stavros' relationship," Elspeth said. "And for what it's worth, I'm sorry. I never intended to do those things, but we were having to stall for time. It was either that, or what I found for the Feds wasn't going to be good enough to put him away."

I opened my mouth and then closed it, unsure of what to say.

"I guess had I known that you were who you were a long time ago, I might've been able to work with you." She sighed. "I still feel like you have no clue how much you helped me. When Daddy saw that I was being 'pursued' by another man, he started to let his guard down."

That was true.

Had I known that she was a willing informant, this could've gone a whole lot smoother.

But I hadn't.

"I...I don't know what to say," I admitted.

She smiled. It was a different smile than the one she used to give me.

"Just say that whatever you found you'll give over to the Feds when they ask for it," she said as she wiped her hands off. "And ask your girl to forgive me."

I nodded.

"My father was an asshole."

I agreed. "He was."

"We really are a lot alike, you know. We both have daddy issues." She bared her teeth. "When I was twenty, I met Stavros. He was a new bodyguard for me." She smiled. "I didn't know why I needed one, but I never complained. I thought I was just a military brat who might've caught the attention of one of my father's enemies. It never occurred to me that it was my father who was bad. Not until mine and Stavros' relationship turned into something more, and my father nearly killed him."

I grunted.

Yeah, sounded like we both had daddy issues.

"One day, Stavros and I were wonderful. The next, Stavros and I were no longer an item. I couldn't understand why. Not until years later when I finally got Stavros to tell me the truth…which was round about the time I started to get curious about some of my observations about my father and his military career."

She looked at her father's body.

"Stavros had changed from the man that I'd fallen in love with. And that change had everything to do with my father. Stavros was forced to do things he never wanted to do, and if he didn't do them, my father threatened the one thing that could keep him doing them. Me."

"Asshole."

"Right?" Elspeth said. "So, Stavros and I went to someone that could help. An FBI agent named Lynn. Stavros knew him from somewhere, and though it'd been a very long time since they'd spoken, he hoped that connection was still there. And it was. Which led us to gather as much evidence as we could. Stavros' job was to do what he was told to do within reason."

Within reason. I smirked.

Her eyes narrowed. "You almost killed him today, though."

I held my hand up. "I didn't know. I was just protecting Janie."

Elspeth smiled sadly. "We knew the risks."

They had. And, so did he.

Which was why he was no longer going to play this dangerous game. He was done. D.O.N.E.

Starting now.

I nodded. She didn't need to justify her reasons for doing what she did. I agreed wholeheartedly based solely on my own convictions.

"You mind untying me?"

Elspeth jumped. "Yes, sorry. I meant to do that earlier. Your face is still bleeding, too. I'm sorry about that. Stavros was supposed to stop any of this from happening. But then your friend showed, and started causing some chaos."

We both looked over at Trace, who at some point in this discussion had blended into the woodwork. He'd been paying attention, but he hadn't said a word.

"I don't really know what you wanted me to do here. Layton told me to come with a gun pointed at my head," Trace pointed out.

I sighed and turned back to Elspeth expectantly.

"Let's do it," I ordered, wiggling my free hand at her.

She untied me, then Trace, moments later.

"I need to call Janie," I said as I reached for my phone that was sitting on the counter next to the scalpel Layton had used to cut my face.

She answered on the first ring.

"We heard," Janie said as she answered the phone. "Elliott just went outside to tell the officers. He said someone will be on their way to come get you momentarily."

I looked at my watch. "I have my own ride when this is finally all sorted out here."

And I did.

Trace was going to take me home in his truck—which I'd seen

outside when 'Stavros' had parked the van next to it.

Then I wasn't going to have another damn thing to do with him for a very, very long time.

Out of everyone that could've told me the truth, I expected it most from him. He'd been my longest standing friend. The one man that had been there from the very beginning.

"I'll be home in a little while," I said, smiling then.

Why did it not surprise me that she knew I'd been watching her?

***

"For what it's worth," Trace said, "I didn't want to go. It was either bring you there, or they take my woman. And, now that you have Janie…you know that you'll always choose her."

I did know.

Which was what sucked.

I couldn't blame him for going and giving up my location.

He'd called earlier and asked where I was while I was in the shower. I'd told him, and hadn't thought another thing of it.

"And your wife? She's okay?"

"I left her there and drove myself to the lovely Casa De Crazy. They said if I cooperated, then she wouldn't be hurt."

I nodded and opened the door, stepping out.

"Rafe?"

I looked over my shoulder at him.

"Yeah?"

"I'm here if you need me."

I snorted. "I won't."

Then I slammed the door in his face.

I walked up my driveway, past a cop, and through my front door.

Before I could close it behind me, Janie was in my arms.

She was there for about point five seconds before she let go of me, and then dashed outside.

Frowning, I turned to look at her, only to get an eyeful of her ass as she bent over into the grass and lost her lunch.

CHAPTER 24

I'm not above biting someone to win an argument.
-Janie's secret thoughts

Janie

"There are some things I've been dying to know."

Rafe's eyes were closed.

He had butterfly bandages all along the length of his cheek. Seven in total.

We were talking. About nothing really in particular, but neither one of us had really gotten over today yet.

It'd been bad.

It'd could've gone way worse than it had, and we were lucky that all had turned out as it had.

Though I was still quite baffled about Elspeth.

Plot twist.

"What do you want to know?" Rafe asked.

I smiled.

"I want to know what makes you tick. I want to know why you're so complicated. I want to know why there are shadows in your eyes. I want to know everything there is to know about the mysterious Raphael Luis," I whispered.

Rafe's eyes opened and went soft.

"I'm a simple man, Janie. I'm a man that lives hard. I'm a man that plays hard. And I'm a man that loves you."

My mouth fell open, but he wasn't done.

"I'm mysterious because by being mysterious, it gives me what I want faster. People always wonder about me, and that makes them careful. Careful means they'll think twice before they fuck with me. And I don't want to have to fuck anyone up. I'm over those days. I just want to be me. I want to live a life where I don't have to look over my shoulder. I want to be Rafe Luis. Not Raphael the douchebag's son that scammed hundreds of people out of their life savings."

I swallowed at the pain I read in his eyes.

"Rafe, you were a child," I started. "When I was three, my father shot a guy that was holding a man hostage. That man had a son who was with him, but that son was cowering in the corner right along with the woman and child he was holding at gunpoint. Do you think that kid is responsible for what his father did?"

"That kid didn't live off of the money the father made while those families went bankrupt," he countered.

I narrowed my eyes. "You paid every cent back that your father stole."

His mouth fell open. Obviously, he didn't know that his sister had shared that information.

I grinned.

"Raven's been talking," he surmised.

"Raven and I have been talking," I acknowledged. "But it's literally one of the only ways I learn about you."

He moved so fast that my breath caught in my throat.

"Anything you want from me, all you have to do is ask," he said. "And I'd appreciate it if the next time someone tells you something's wrong with me, that you share. Just like I'd want you to share something about you if you knew it."

My brows rose. "I honestly thought that you did know."

He sighed. "I don't have any idea how that was kept from me by goddamn everyone. For fucking months. But it would've been nice to know that was why you were rushing rushing until life was no fun."

I rolled my eyes. "That was another song from before my time, old man."

He grinned. "'I'm In a Hurry' by Alabama is good stuff. Which, you obviously know seeing as you understood the lyrics I spouted."

I moved my hand up his side, and then stopped when I reached his armpit.

Then another familiar bout of nausea rose up, and I pushed him. "Oh God. Get up."

He moved fast, looking around the room for the threat.

I launched myself off the bed while he was searching, and then nearly tripped over both dogs that were lying on my side of the bed.

I made it to the bathroom but didn't make it to the toilet.

Unfortunately, I threw up on the towel that he'd laid down to dry up the water that had dripped off of us after our shower together.

"Are you sure there's nothing you want to tell me?"

I smiled, despite feeling another wave of nausea hit me. "Your dinner of pizza and breadsticks doesn't agree with your baby."

"My baby?" he drawled. "What about your baby?"

I shrugged and stood up as the wave left me.

Moments later, I squatted down and gathered the towel, folding it in on itself, then placing it in the hamper.

I'd take care of it after I brushed my teeth and washed my hands.

Only, when I finished those two tasks, I found myself turned around with my ass sitting on the wet bathroom counter.

"When were you going to tell me?" He moved in until his mouth was inches from mine.

His eyes were full of desire, and happiness.

So happy.

I felt my eyes well with tears.

"I didn't know until my dad suggested I get it together. I walked into the bathroom after you were gone, came back out, and Elliott teasingly asked me if I was pregnant to lighten the mood."

Rafe's face transformed as a brilliant smile took over his face.

One that quickly fell.

"I don't know how to be a good dad. I didn't have one to show me how," he admitted.

I waved him away.

"I got a good one. You have a few months to learn from him."

He leaned forward and pressed a kiss to my nose.

Moments later, I had my legs around his hips as he carried me to his bed, laid me down, then proceeded to make sweet love to me.

Hours later, as I was drifting to sleep, I felt something cool and hard slip on my ring finger.

"You're supposed to ask, silly."

He snorted. "Asking would imply that there was an option for you to say no. There's not."

I snorted.

Then fell off into sleep, happier than I'd ever been in my life.

Which was saying something, because I had a lot of happy.

EPILOGUE

She's actually a very nice person once you feed her.
-Rafe when introducing Janie

Rafe

2 months later

This dress was everything.

My breath caught, and I stared as everything I ever imagined walked toward me down the aisle.

She was wearing a beautiful floor-length white dress. It was big, poofy, and reminded me of one of those Barbie dresses that were meant to be over the top.

The elegant train followed behind her and extended at least five feet in length.

She wasn't wearing a veil at my request.

I wanted to see her eyes the moment she saw me.

I still had the flask of whiskey in my pocket, but that was for later when the party started.

I didn't usually drink all that much, but a man should drink a little bit on his wedding night, right?

Janie's eyes finally moved up and caught mine, and the smile she aimed in my direction was one that stole the oxygen from my lungs.

Her father, who was at her side, chuckled at my expression.

I felt like I'd been poleaxed.

She was so fucking beautiful that it hurt.

And I was one lucky SOB.

"Who gives this woman away?"

Janie's father swallowed once. "Her mother and I do."

Janie hiccupped.

And I knew then and there that her wedding photos would show that there hadn't been but one dry eye in the house—mine.

Because I wouldn't cry.

And not because a man didn't cry.

Because I had her. I had our baby. I had everything.

My hand closed around hers, and I pulled her closer to me.

She smiled and came, not resisting at all.

And moments later, when the preacher asked if I took this woman, I said two of the most important words in the English language. "I do."

Janie

6 months later

I opened my eyes and found a pair of scuffed motorcycle boots kicked up on the end of my bed.

I smiled at seeing Rafe's feet there, mostly because it meant he'd gone to sleep finally.

He'd been up all night with me and then had stayed up even longer when I'd finally passed out due to exhaustion after giving birth, to care for our new baby girl.

I grinned at his exhausted slump.

"Remember holding you like this like it was yesterday," Dad said, drawing my attention away from Rafe's boots to him.

I smiled.

"I was never that small, surely," I teased.

"Smaller," Dad said. "You used to fit into two of my hands. Your chunk doesn't quite fit."

He showed me how she was overflowing his two hands.

I smiled.

My child was indeed a chunk.

A fat, roly-poly little perfect girl that I loved with all my heart already, and she was only a few hours old.

She looked exactly like her daddy.

She had an uncontrollable head full of black hair, tan skin, and the perfect bow-shaped lips that would grow into every girl's dream lips one day.

Her eyes were a dark bluish gray, and I had no doubt in my mind that they'd turn even darker like her father's since it seemed his genes were dominant.

"She's a chunk for sure," I agreed. "But she's a short chunk. She was about eighteen and a half inches. They said she was short and fat."

"She is," he agreed. "And adorable."

I felt my heart fill with love at the sight of grandfather and granddaughter.

"So how does it feel to be a granddad, Dad?" I smiled.

My dad sighed. "It feels like the whole fuckin' world was handed to me all over again."

My eyes filled with tears. "I completely agree with you."

Twenty-four and a half years ago, he'd said the same thing about me the moment I was placed in his arms. And, when I'd held our little miracle in my own arms for the first time, I'd realized what my father meant when he'd said that to me when I told him I was pregnant.

"Your whole life will change. One second you'll be just you, and the next your every thought will be of her. You won't know how to function without first thinking about her."

"I love you, Daddy."

My father dropped his lips to the top of Abrielle's head. "I love you, too, baby girl."

ABOUT THE AUTHOR

Lani Lynn Vale is married to the love of her life that she met in high school. She fell in love with him because he was wearing baseball pants. Ten years later they have three perfectly crazy children and a cat named Demon who likes to wake her up at ungodly times in the night. They live in the greatest state in the world, Texas. She writes contemporary and romantic suspense, and has a love for all things romance. You can find Lani in front of her computer writing away in her fictional characters' world...that is until her husband and kids demand sustenance in the form of food and drink.